The Lost Treasure of Casa Loma

THE TOM AUSTEN MYSTERIES
by Eric Wilson

Terror in Winnipeg
Murder on *The Canadian*
Vancouver Nightmare
The Ghost of Lunenburg Manor

A TOM AUSTEN MYSTERY

The Lost Treasure of Casa Loma

ERIC WILSON

Stoddart Kids

For my friends in England
The Tinkers and Brian Atkinson
Tom Oldroyd and Curt Noel

First published in 1982 by General Paperbacks
Published in 1992 by Stoddart Publishing Co. Limited

Published in Canada in 1997 by
Stoddart Kids,
a division of Stoddart Publishing Co. Ltd.
895 Don Mills Road, 400-2 Park Centre
Toronto, Canada M3C 1W3
Tel (416) 445-3333 Fax (416) 445-5967
E-mail cservice@genpub.com

Published in the United States in 1997 by
Stoddart Kids,
a division of Stoddart Publishing Co. Ltd.
180 Varick Street, 9th Floor
New York, New York 10014
Toll free 1-800-805-1083
E-mail gdsinc@genpub.com

Distributed in Canada by
General Distribution Services
325 Humber College Blvd.
Toronto, Canada M9W 7C3
Tel (416) 213-1919 Fax (416) 213-1917
E-mail cservice@genpub.com

Distributed in the United States by
General Distribution Services, PMB 128
4500 Witmer Industrial Estates
Niagara Falls, New York 14305-1386
Toll free 1-800-805-1083
E-mail gdsinc@genpub.com

05 04 03 02 01 7 8 9 10 11

Canadian Cataloguing in Publication Data

Wilson, Eric
The lost treasure of Casa Loma
6th ed.
(A Tom and Liz Austen mystery)

ISBN 0-7736-7492-6

1. Casa Loma (Toronto, Ont.) — Juvenile fiction. I. Title.
II. Series: Wilson, Eric. A Tom and Liz Austen mystery.

PS8595.I583L68 2001   jC813'.54   C2001-93026-8
PZ7.W6935Lo 2001

*We acknowledge for their financial support of our publishing program the
Government of Canada through the Book Publishing Industry Development
Program (BPIDP), the Canada Council, and the Ontario Arts Council.*

Cover design: Brant Cowie/ArtPlus Limited
Cover illustration: Albert Slark

Printed and bound in Canada

CASA LOMA

KENSINGTON MARKET

BASEBALL STADIUM

ONTARIO PLACE

FORT YORK

TORONTO

LAKE ONTARIO

Niagara River

USA

CANADA

Rainbow Bridge

The Falls

FIRST FLOOR OF CASA LOMA

Great Hall

Study

Billiard Room

Entrance

Library

Conservatory

Peacock Alley

I

'We fear it was murder.'

The butler's gloomy face was lit by a flash of lightning from the storm outside. 'But please come in. Mr Winter will tell you all the details about Sir Nigel's disappearance.'

Tom shivered with excitement as he stepped into Casa Loma, a castle in the heart of Toronto. He put down his suitcase and followed his sister Liz and their Uncle Henry to the castle's Great Hall.

A log fire roared, throwing an orange light on suits of armour and crossed lances on the walls.

'Welcome to Toronto, Mr Austen.' A handsome dark-haired man came forward. 'I'm Vince Winter, a close friend of Sir Nigel's.'

After the introductions were over, Uncle Henry went to the enormous fireplace to warm his hands.

'This is a sad occasion. I was very fond of Sir Nigel.'

Vince looked thoughtfully into the flames. 'We don't know that he's actually dead.'

'What happened?'

'I'll tell you in just a minute. First, if I may, let me introduce Sir Nigel's private secretary.'

A young woman in a wheelchair came across the Great Hall toward them. 'I'm Tia Nightingale, Mr Austen.'

'Please, Tia, first names only.'

She smiled. 'That's a nice idea. But you may get objections from the new butler, Smythe. He's only been at Casa Loma a few days, and seems a bit stuffy.'

Tom glanced toward a distant corner of the Great Hall, where the butler stood under a carving of an evil-eyed jester. Had he heard what Tia had said?

Vince motioned to Smythe. 'Sherry, please, and Cokes for Tom and Liz.'

'Very good, sir.'

Vince led Uncle Henry through a doorway. 'This is the library. Let's have our sherry in here, while I tell you as much as I know about what happened to Sir Nigel.'

Smythe appeared with a silver tray, and passed around the drinks. Tia sipped hers cautiously, then nodded. 'I'm pleased this is actually sherry. Yesterday Smythe served us brandy by mistake.'

Tom thanked the butler for his Coke, and accepted a tiny sandwich served by a pretty maid. Then he waited impatiently for details of Sir Nigel's mysterious disappearance, which had brought Uncle

Henry to Casa Loma. He and Liz had been staying with their uncle when the news had arrived, and had been excited by the prospect of accompanying him to Toronto.

But, before anyone could speak, a thin man of about sixty came into the library and approached Uncle Henry. 'May we have a word in private, Mr Austen?'

'We don't have any secrets out West, where I come from. Please speak your piece.'

The thin man swallowed nervously, and glanced toward Smythe. 'My name is Hatfield, and I am Sir Nigel's valet. I have been in his service for many years now. Is it correct you are taking over Casa Loma?'

Uncle Henry nodded, and his glasses caught the light. 'Sir Nigel is my cousin. If he can't be found, I shall inherit the castle.'

'Then, sir, I must warn you something is terribly wrong here! Some of the new servants, including Smythe, don't even know their jobs. But it's the stables I must tell you about. I . . .'

At that moment the lights went out. Startled cries sounded in the room, then Smythe's reassuring voice was heard.

'The storm must have blown down the power lines,' he said. 'I'll fetch some candles.'

Suffocating darkness filled the library, and Tom's nerves prickled with tension as the minutes passed. Why was Smythe taking so long?

At last a match flared into life and the yellow light of several candles cut the darkness, revealing the shadowed faces of the assembled company.

'Well, Hatfield?' Uncle Henry said, looking around for the valet. 'What were you saying?'

'He's not here, Unc,' Liz said.

'But where has he gone?'

'Let's not worry about Hatfield now,' Vince said. 'I was just about to tell you what happened to Sir Nigel. Come along, and I'll show you the room where he disappeared.' Picking up a candlestick, he led the way to a long dark hallway. 'This is called Peacock Alley. Over here is the door to Sir Nigel's study. Nothing in it has been moved since he disappeared.'

Opening the door, Vince stepped into the study. Then he gasped. 'Oh no! It can't be!'

The horror in his voice made Tom's hair stand on end. Stepping closer, he looked into the study. Sprawled on the floor, the twisted features of his face yellow in the candlelight, was Hatfield.

2

'Everyone get back!'

Vince slammed the study door closed and gestured to the maid. 'Irene, go and phone the police!'

'Yes, Mr Winter.'

'I insist we all wait together here until the police arrive.'

Tom nodded his head in agreement as he glanced around at the other faces in the yellow candlelight. Had one of them attacked Hatfield and dragged him to the study while the lights were out? Obviously Uncle Henry and Liz were not involved, but that still left several other suspects.

'Mr Winter!' Irene called, hurrying back toward them along Peacock Alley. 'The phone is dead, so I can't call the police.'

'Surely the storm hasn't affected the phone as well?'

'Perhaps someone cut the line. Could that be possible?'

'That's *very* possible, Irene.' For several long moments Vince gazed thoughtfully at the young woman, until finally she dropped her eyes. 'Well, I'd better drive to police headquarters and make a full report. But, first, we'll have to find out what happened to Hatfield.'

Tom edged closer, his heart beating rapidly as he watched Vince reopen the study door and look inside.

The room was empty.

'That's impossible!' Tom said, staring into the study. 'There's only the one door, and no windows!'

Suddenly the lights came back on and everyone crowded into the room, staring at the place where they had seen Hatfield's body only a few moments before.

'We can't *all* be crazy!' Vince said, trying to smile. 'I'm sure the police will find an explanation. But, first, let's go back into the library so I can tell Henry and the kids about what happened to Sir Nigel.'

Tia shivered as she turned her wheelchair to leave the study. 'A second mysterious disappearance within a few days. I think I'll look for another job.'

'Please don't,' Uncle Henry said, walking beside her into the library. 'I'd be lost, trying to run this place alone.'

Vince sat down and stretched his long legs, then looked at his digital watch. 'I'm sorry, it's getting late, but I do want you to hear about Sir Nigel.'

Uncle Henry tried to smile. 'Yes, we'd better hear quickly, before someone else disappears.'

Tia leaned forward in her wheelchair. 'As you know, Sir Nigel Brampton purchased Casa Loma a year ago, after retiring here from Britain. The castle cost a mint, but Sir Nigel had earned millions from oil and gold.'

Vince smiled. 'Millions? I'd have said jillions, or maybe zillions.'

'Sir Nigel was fascinated by the history of Casa Loma and tried to find out as much about it as he could. One unusual thing he learned was that the original owner was so horse-crazy that he had false teeth made for a favourite charger, but that's not . . .'

'Excuse me,' Liz said. 'I'm a horse freak, too. Did the false teeth work?'

'I don't know,' Tia answered, smiling. 'Anyway, one day Sir Nigel discovered an old coded document. When he broke the code, it led him to a cache of hidden diamonds.'

'Diamonds! How fabulous!'

'Fabulous is right. I saw them once, shortly before Sir Nigel hid them again, and they were gorgeous. Tiny, radiant perfection.'

Uncle Henry frowned. 'You say he *hid* them again?'

'Yes. Sir Nigel wouldn't trust a safety-deposit box, so he found a new hiding-place in Casa Loma.'

Vince gulped down the last of his sherry. 'Shortly afterwards, I was introduced to Sir Nigel by Tia, and we became close friends. I urged him to put the diamonds in a bank, but he refused.'

Tia shook her head. 'That was a mistake. The police are convinced it's criminals after the diamonds who are behind Sir Nigel's disappearance.'

'Exactly what happened?'

'A week ago, Sir Nigel was working in his study. A maid had just taken him a cup of tea when she heard a terrible cry. Rushing back to the study, she found Sir Nigel lying face-down across his desk, apparently dead or at least unconscious.'

Vince shuddered with the memory. 'I was a weekend guest of Sir Nigel's at the time. When the maid raised the alarm, I rushed to the study and . . .'

'Yes?'

'And the study was empty.'

'Just as it was with Hatfield!'

'Exactly. Sir Nigel disappeared into thin air, and not one word has been heard from him since.'

For a moment no one spoke. Tom glanced at Liz, wondering what his sister thought about the strange events at Casa Loma. Suddenly there was a loud crash somewhere in the castle.

Vince smiled. 'Don't worry, Casa Loma doesn't have ghosts. Sometimes the wind slams a door.'

'What about that horrible creaking?' Liz asked.

'That's only the teak floors.'

'Are you sure? It sounds more like a pack of zombies roaming around.'

Vince smiled, then turned to Uncle Henry. 'And so, as Sir Nigel's closest relative, you have been summoned from Winnipeg to look after Casa Loma. Should Sir Nigel not be found, the castle will be yours.'

A mournful grandfather clock tolled midnight.

Uncle Henry ran his hand nervously through his hair.

'Sir Nigel had better be found. This castle gives me the creeps.'

The next morning Tom felt groggy. He hadn't slept well, despite the luxury of a massive bed in The Round Room, which, Vince had told him, had once been occupied by the Duke of Windsor.

He went down to the Great Hall in search of breakfast, and found Liz already there combing her hair in front of a gold-framed mirror.

'Guess what?' she said happily. 'The shower in my suite has perfumed water.'

'My bathroom's so big, I could use a bike to get around it. But there's only a bathtub.'

'One of the servants told me Sir Nigel's private suite has a fabulous shower with six taps. Apparently Sir Nigel never bothered using it, but I'm sure no one would object if you tried it.'

'Good idea.'

Smythe appeared. 'Breakfast is served, young sir and madam.'

The butler's glum face was an upsetting reminder of Hatfield's disappearance the night before. The castle was spooky even in daylight; Tom and Liz followed Smythe into the breakfast room, where Uncle Henry was eating a huge serving of bacon and eggs while talking to the young maid, Irene.

'Good morning, kids! How'd you sleep?'

'So-so,' Tom said, sitting down in a gigantic chair carved with sea serpents and dragons. 'Have the police arrived yet?'

'Not yet. Vince drove down to make a report last night after you'd gone to bed. They'll probably be here later this morning.'

'Great! I can't wait.'

Uncle Henry smiled, looking a bit sheepish. 'I hate to be a killjoy, but I've already made plans with Irene for your morning. You've only got a week's spring holiday from school, so I figured you'd want to explore Toronto before you fly home.'

Irene grinned at Tom and Liz. 'How about us seeing a human scalp this morning?'

'Hey!' Tom said. 'That sounds all right!'

Just then, Tia entered the room in her wheelchair. 'Planning to visit Fort York? I'd enjoy showing you round. Before my accident, I was a guide there.'

'Then take the morning off,' Uncle Henry said. 'With Smythe and twenty-five servants, the castle should survive! Right, Smythe?'

The butler nodded solemnly. Dark circles under his eyes, and several shaving cuts on his chin, made him an unattractive sight this morning. Tom was glad Smythe wasn't going to Fort York with them.

The first sight of the fort was a Union Jack, being tossed by the cold, rainy wind. As they drove into the parking lot, they heard a cannon boom.

'Want some help?' Tom asked, as Tia wrestled her wheelchair out of Irene's car.

'No thanks, I'm used to this. I drive myself to work, using hand controls.'

Tia wheeled the chair toward the fort, leaving two long tracks behind her on the muddy path. 'During the War of 1812,' she explained to Tom and Liz, 'American forces invaded this area. Fort York was the headquarters of the British defenders.'

Irene smiled. 'These days, the American invaders are all tourists.'

'And some of us like Canada so much, we stay.'

'Are you from the USA then, Tia?'

She nodded. 'Look, there's the Fort York guard, drilling with Brown Bess muskets. Aren't their red uniforms splendid?'

'Where's that scalp?'

'Follow me,' Irene said, laughing.

The scalp—long black hair and a bit of skin attached to a wooden stretcher—was displayed inside a barracks. Satisfied now he had seen it, Tom followed the others to the fort's magazine to see a shot-oven. This, Tia told them, had been used for heating cannon-balls to set enemy ships on fire.

Next, they went into the officers' kitchen, where an aproned girl was making cinnamon doughnuts over an open fire. Copper pots reflected the flickering flames, and the circles of sizzling dough made Tom's mouth water.

The girl gave each of them a doughnut, and Tom wandered outside eating his.

Hatfield was standing in the yard.

Tom nearly choked on his doughnut. He hurried toward the man.

'Hatfield! You're alive!'

The man's face went white when he saw Tom. He turned to the two small children at his side. 'Go and find Granny. I'll be there in a minute.'

When the children were gone, he looked at Tom. 'O.K., so I'm Hatfield. What of it?'

'What happened last night? And what were you going to say about the stables?'

'Just that the blacksmith was pounding cold iron. Now, please, leave me alone.'

Hatfield started away, but Tom followed. 'What happened to you after the lights went out?'

Hatfield's face was marked by tension. 'Listen to me. They've threatened my family if I talk to anyone about Casa Loma. So please get away from me.'

'*Who* threatened you?'

Hatfield stared at Tom with fear written plainly on his face, then he hurried toward the parking lot. Puzzled, Tom watched him get into a car with a woman and the two young children.

After making a note of the car's number, Tom walked thoughtfully back toward the officers' quarters. He was greatly relieved to discover that Hatfield had not been murdered the night before, but he was completely mystified by the strange events that had happened at Casa Loma.

Speaking of the castle, what was all this about a blacksmith? Tom stopped to jot *blacksmith pounding cold iron* in his notebook, then continued on with a big smile on his face.

Excellent lead!

3

'Guess what?' Tom said, as the others came out of the officers' quarters. 'Hatfield is alive!'

'What?' Tia exclaimed. 'You must be joking!'

'Nope. He was right here at Fort York, large as life and happy as a clam. Happy, that is, until I gave him the third degree and he spilled a clue that points me straight at a major suspect.'

'A suspect? Who is it?'

'I shouldn't say, in case my man's innocent and I ruin his reputation.'

Tia studied Tom's face thoughtfully. 'I admire that.' She wheeled her chair toward the parking lot. The others followed, and they were soon heading back to the castle.

The towers of Casa Loma were magnificent as they approached. 'What a sight!' Liz said. 'Unless the crooks have found them, the diamonds must be hidden in one of the castle's ninety-eight rooms. I wonder which one?'

Tia brushed back her thick curls. 'Sir Nigel once teased me with a clue, but I couldn't figure it out.'

'A clue! Please tell us.'

'These were his exact words: "It's the same place as pictures are sent, when they've made a mess of things."'

'Weird.'

Once back at the castle, Tom and Liz found Uncle Henry in the billiard room. They told him about Hatfield, but he was as puzzled as they were by the man's strange behaviour. Although the police still had not arrived to investigate yesterday evening's events, the morning had been busy, and unpleasant, for Uncle Henry.

'The servants are complaining about Smythe, and threatening to quit if the old butler doesn't return.'

'But where is he?'

'No one knows. He left shortly after Sir Nigel disappeared, and Smythe came as his replacement. According to the other servants, Smythe is making a mess of running things.'

'Why don't you boot him out?'

Uncle Henry made an unhappy face. 'I tried to, Liz, but then I just couldn't do it. I talked to Smythe, said he had to leave, and the poor man was so upset that I changed my mind. But I warned him he'll have to shape up or ship out.'

Liz smiled. 'Get on the ball, Smythe, or get on the boat.'

'You bet!' Uncle Henry said, trying to look stern.

'Say Unc, may we explore the castle's towers?'

'Sure.' Uncle Henry leaned over the billiard table to take a shot. 'Let's ask Smythe to take us. It might cheer him up.'

Not long afterwards, they were climbing the stairs which spiralled up inside a gloomy tower. Tom half expected to be attacked by bats, and was pleased to step out into the open air.

'Be careful,' Smythe warned as they approached the stone rampart around the roof. 'The rain has made it slippery up here.'

'Far-out view,' Liz said, looking at the city's office towers standing along the shore of Lake Ontario. 'This was a great place to build a castle.'

'Casa Loma is Spanish for "the house on the hill".'

'Some house!'

Tom and Liz crossed over to the other side of the tower roof. Leaning over the rampart, they looked down at the red tiles and stone unicorns below.

'Those must be the stables,' Tom whispered, pointing at a distant building. 'Got time to investigate them?'

'Because of what Hatfield told you?'

'Yes. He said that . . .'

Suddenly there was a terrible cry. Whirling around, Tom saw Uncle Henry and Smythe struggling at the edge of the rampart. For an awful moment Tom thought Smythe was trying to push Uncle Henry over. Then he realized that in fact the butler had kept his uncle from falling. Tom ran to help, but before he reached him, Uncle Henry had managed to scramble back to safety.

'I almost fell! I leaned against the rampart and a stone slipped. Thank heavens, Smythe, that you were right beside me!'

A closer look revealed a loose stone in the rampart. Uncle Henry seemed satisfied that this had caused the nearly fatal accident, but Tom still kept a long way from Smythe as they descended the tower's narrow stairs.

'Let's try those stables,' Tom whispered to Liz, when they were alone.

It was now pouring with rain and the water bounced off the road as Tom and Liz ran to the stables.

'I'm soaked!' Liz said, wiping her foggy glasses. 'We should have asked the chauffeur to drive us over.'

Tom laughed. 'This rich life suits you, Liz. Soon you'll be taking baths in milk.'

Liz glanced into a feed room, but it was empty and cobwebs were thick in the corners. 'The stables must be . . . Yikes!'

A huge man appeared from round a dark corner. For a moment he stared at them with unsmiling eyes. 'Get out of here,' he said, gesturing menacingly with an enormous hand.

'Hey!' Tom protested. 'We want to see the stables.' When there was no reply he swallowed nervously and added, 'Please.'

'There's nothing to see. The horses are still at winter quarters in southern USA.'

'Oh, well,' Liz shrugged. 'We'd better come back

with Uncle Henry. You'll let your new boss look around, won't you?'

The man looked hostile. After a moment, he pointed down a dark passage. 'Follow that and you'll find the horse stalls.'

'Thanks.'

Tom and Liz stumbled along the dark passage as directed but it only lead to a blank wall. Returning, they heard the sound of metal ringing against metal and followed it to a large room containing two rows of enclosed horse stalls. Near a forge, the unfriendly blacksmith was pounding a horseshoe on the anvil. Tom shivered, wishing there was a fire in the forge to warm the chilly air.

'Let's go!' he shouted to Liz above the noise of the blacksmith's ringing blows.

As they reached the outside door, footsteps sounded from the dark passage and a man came out, carrying a tray of steaming food. It was the chauffeur who'd met them at the airport yesterday.

'Oh!' he said. 'You startled me! I, uh, brought my lunch over from Casa Loma. I like eating in private.'

'How about a ride home after you've eaten?'

The chauffeur smiled, but a nerve twitched in his eyelid. 'Afraid not, Miss. The limousine's parked at the castle.'

'Oh, your clothes are dry, so I thought you must have driven over here.'

The chauffeur mumbled something over his shoulder as he headed for the horse stalls. Outside, Liz turned her rain-streaked face to look back at the stables.

'Did you notice the horses' names in gold on the doors of the horse stalls? I bet there's enough room inside those fancy stalls for a horse to entertain several friends to tea.'

'All I noticed was that blacksmith's arms. If the diamonds are hidden under the castle, he could just lift it up for us. I wonder why he lied to us about where the horse stalls were?'

Tom had been planning to question the blacksmith about what Hatfield had said concerning the stables, but one look at those muscles and the plan had evaporated. Embarrassed by this failure, and feeling miserable after the rain, he decided to drown his blues in a hot shower.

Remembering what Liz had told him about the fabulous shower in Sir Nigel's private suite, he headed there after receiving permission from Uncle Henry.

His footsteps were silenced by a thick carpet as he approached the suite. He stopped in surprise at the doorway, for there, standing beside a table and holding a photograph in a silver picture-frame, was the maid, Irene.

For a moment, she didn't notice Tom, and he didn't speak. After studying the photograph for a few moments, Irene put it down and turned toward the door.

'Tom! What a scare you gave me! I, um, I was just checking that everything was O.K. in here.'

Tom glanced toward the wooden bedstead, carved with forked-tongued serpents. 'But it hasn't been used for a week.'

Irene smiled, and pushed her black hair back off

her face. 'You're right. Actually, I was walking past the room and saw the secret panel was open. I came in to close it, and noticed that photograph of Sir Nigel and your uncle.'

'A secret panel! May I see it?'

Irene went to the fireplace. 'There's a button hidden under the mantel. You just push it, and presto.'

A thin panel beside the fireplace swung open, revealing narrow shelves holding books and papers. 'Disappointed?' Irene said, smiling. 'I bet you expected to see the diamonds.'

Tom smiled. 'This secret panel hardly seems secret.'

'You're right. All the servants know about it, but I wonder who opened it, and why.'

When Irene had left, Tom went into Sir Nigel's bathroom. The marble walls were streaked with colours, and the many fixtures included a telephone linked to the castle's private phone system.

Dropping his clothes on the floor, Tom stepped into the shower. Six separate taps controlled the spray from silver rails which enclosed him. The hot, stinging water coming at him from all directions was so invigorating that Tom began to sing.

Perhaps in protest, the main pipe clunked loudly and the water died to a trickle. Unable to get the water flowing again, Tom grabbed a fluffy towel and rubbed his hair until it stood up in red spikes.

Then he noticed that a tube of Sir Nigel's toothpaste had been cut neatly in half. The toothpaste had been squeezed out and hadn't yet hardened. It looked as if someone had suspected this was the hiding-place for the diamonds—someone who had very recently left the bathroom.

A shiver passed through Tom. Close by in the castle there was someone, perhaps well known to Tom, who was behind the disappearance of Sir Nigel and the determined search for the diamonds.

But who?

4

Vince and Tom walked along a street, jostled by the shoppers crowding Toronto's Kensington Market. Vince bought two Jamaican hot beef patties, and Tom ate his while he tried to puzzle out a meat market sign reading *Grande Especial Carne de Porco*.

'Big special on pork chops, I guess. What language is that?'

'Portuguese. Toronto is home to people from all over the world, including yours truly. I'm from San Francisco.'

Tom looked in the door of a record shop, where music blasted out and a straw-hatted clerk danced behind the counter. The boy gave Tom a friendly wave inviting him to join him, but Tom shyly shook his head and hurried on.

'Sir Nigel moved here from Britain. Maybe that was a mistake.'

Vince shook his head. 'His mistake was hiding those diamonds in Casa Loma. He trusted people not to be greedy.'

A sweaty teenager came their way, trundling a cart loaded with red snappers on ice; as the fish passed, their huge, dead eyes seemed to stare at Tom. 'That's as creepy a sight as the face on that Casa Loma blacksmith. There's something strange happening in the stables, Vince. I'm going to poke around there this evening.'

'So you said earlier. And I repeat my warning: don't chance it.'

Tom bent to rub the head of a mongrel sprawled in a doorway. 'Why'd you move here from the USA, Vince?'

'I was offered a sportscasting job by a local TV station. I'm pleased to say sky-rocketing ratings have followed.'

'Which sports?'

'You name it, I report it. Most of the pro athletes in town are close buddies of mine.'

'Hey, neat! Like who?'

'Dexter Valentine, for one.'

'What! Dexter Valentine is your friend? I don't believe it!'

'Then why don't I prove it?' Vince crossed the road between a van unloading olive oil that was blocking the narrow street and a tiny car, which was beeping its squeaky horn in protest. 'Let's ring this doorbell, and see if Dexter's home.'

Tom waited, doubtful that the famous shortstop

for the Toronto Blue Jays baseball team would really open the door.

When he did, Tom's jaw nearly fell off. He was still struggling for speech after he'd been introduced and they'd gone up a flight of stairs to an apartment overlooking the market.

'Liveliest view in town,' Dexter said, leading them to the balcony. 'Plus fresh fruit and vegetables, right on our doorstep.'

Tom tried to think of an intelligent comment, but could only stare in awe at the man. His wife came on to the balcony carrying a baby, and Tom was introduced. The Valentines then produced some refreshments, and Tom gradually began to relax.

'This is delicious,' he said, taking another bite of a crunchy, corn-meal fritter as he looked down at the market.

Vince looked at his watch. 'I should be heading for the TV station soon. Hey, Tom, how about you and Liz coming to tomorrow night's baseball game as my guests?'

'Fantastic!'

'Then, with the Valentines' permission, I'll use their phone to make the arrangements.'

When Vince had left the balcony, Tom worked up enough courage to ask Dexter Valentine how he liked being a star baseball player. The man laughed good-naturedly, and told some fascinating stories about life in professional baseball.

'The player under the most pressure is the pitcher, who's the focus of constant attention. When he has a bad game, and makes such a mess of things that another pitcher must take over, it's a long and unhappy walk to the showers.'

'Wait a minute!' Tom exclaimed. 'That's it!'

'Huh?'

'Tia got it wrong! Sir Nigel didn't say "pictures", he said "pitchers"!'

The Valentines stared in amazement as Tom did a joyful jig around the balcony. Vince returned, and Tom blurted out, 'Guess what? I know where the diamonds are hidden!'

Vince laughed briefly, but then looked thoughtful. 'I believe you mean it.'

Tom grinned happily.

'So? Where are they?'

'I'd rather not say, in case I'm wrong. But let's head for Casa Loma, and I'll test my theory.'

'Hold your horses. We can't just leave in the middle of visiting the Valentines.'

Tom choked back his disappointment as Vince sat down and accepted another cup of coffee from the Valentines, while he explained to the puzzled couple why Tom was so excited. All three then did their best to squeeze the secret out of Tom, but he just grinned and shook his head.

'What if I'm wrong? I'd look like a prize turkey.'

Smiling, Vince stood up. 'It's clear Tom can't be moved, and I must get going. One more phone call, and then we'll say good-bye.'

He was gone some time, and Tom tried to calm his excitement while he bounced the gurgling baby in his arms. But at last Vince was ready to leave, and they were soon hurrying through the market. Tom barely noticed the delicious smells from bakeries and spice sellers in his eagerness to get back to the castle.

'Listen, Tom, I'm already late for an on-air interview with Jacques Savard, the ice hockey player. You'll have to take a streetcar to Casa Loma.'

'Sure, Vince, and thanks. It was great touring the market and meeting the Valentines. Liz made a big mistake, deciding to visit the Science Centre today.'

Several streetcars passed, and Vince grew anxious and impatient as he stared along the street.

'At last! O.K., Tom, this next streetcar is yours. Get out at Prince Edward Drive, and ask someone the way to Casa Loma.' He made sure Tom was safely on board, then waved good-bye. 'I hope you find the diamonds. Save a couple for me!'

Tom walked to a seat at the back of the streetcar as it swayed along the tracks. There was only a handful of other passengers on board; Tom glanced at them, then looked out at some kids playing baseball on a school's concrete playground.

Two men in bulky raincoats and floppy hats were waiting at the next stop. The first dropped into a seat at the front as the second struggled into the streetcar on crutches.

The driver offered to help, but the man shook his head and slowly made his way down the aisle. Tom smiled at his choice of both a raincoat and wrap-around sun-glasses; he was obviously prepared for any weather.

Tom shifted closer to the window as the man sat down heavily beside him. Tom wondered briefly why the man hadn't selected an empty seat, then he looked out of the window at a red push-cart displaying candy apples and hot cashews. A candy apple would be a perfect reward for finding the diamonds; he wished the streetcar would double its speed.

'Pickpocket! Pickpocket!'

The cry came from the man beside Tom. As the streetcar ground to a halt, the other passengers turned round. The man struggled up on to his crutches and pointed an accusing finger at Tom.

'This boy stole my wallet!'

'What?' Tom said in disbelief. 'Are you crazy?'

'It's in your pocket!'

Tom looked down, and was stunned to see a worn leather wallet, clearly visible in his pocket. 'Hey, what . . . ?'

'You sneaky little thief! Stealing from the handicapped! You should be behind bars.'

The other man who'd boarded at the last stop came along the car toward them; close up, the raincoat and hat no longer hid his identity from Tom.

'Hey! You're . . .'

'Just you be quiet,' the man said, his strong voice overpowering Tom's. 'I'm a police officer, son, and you're under arrest.'

'What are you . . . ?'

But again Tom was drowned out as the man called for the driver to open the rear doors. He dragged Tom out of the streetcar and toward a station wagon parked in an alley. Tom looked round desperately for help, but the alley was deserted. Suddenly he found himself being thrown roughly on to the floor of the station wagon, and with a burst of power, it shot off into the traffic.

Fear pounded through Tom as he looked up from the floor and saw the blacksmith from the stables at Casa Loma leaning menacingly over him.

'Don't move, don't speak,' the man said to Tom and then turned toward the driver. 'Better slow down. We don't want to be stopped for speeding, especially after I posed as a cop!'

The station wagon slowed down, and Tom tried to fight his fear by concentrating on the driver, who he couldn't see from the floor. Who was it? Where were they taking him, and why had he been kidnapped?

As the questions whirled inside Tom's head, he began to panic. He closed his eyes, and tried to think about Liz and the others at Casa Loma; when he didn't return, they'd be sure to raise the alarm.

Time passed, and the station wagon rolled on. Tom's eyes grew heavy, and unwillingly he fell into a troubled sleep.

He awoke to find the blacksmith shaking his shoulder. 'Come with me.'

Cold air was blowing in the open door of the station wagon. Tom stumbled out into the black night, and was dragged toward the door of a building. He was bundled down a hallway and shoved into a dark room at the end of it.

The door closed behind him, and a key turned in the lock.

Light seeped around the locked door, outlining chairs and a sofa; in one corner of the dark room Tom could make out a fireplace.

Low voices came from the hallway on the other

side of the door. Tom moved closer, and his stomach tightened in fear as he heard the blacksmith say, 'I'll break that kid. It'll take two seconds, or less.'

There was a reply from a second voice, presumably that of the driver of the station wagon. Tom strained to hear what was said, but the voice was so low it was barely a murmur.

'Not yet,' the blacksmith said. 'First, I'm gonna watch the game on TV.'

The other voice said something which again Tom didn't catch.

'I like him,' the blacksmith said. 'He's got style, with that twenty-four hour watch and everything. I'm getting one of those when he pays me for this job.'

A murmur.

'O.K., so I'm working for *both* of you! Sure, it was you who found out the study has a latch instead of a button, but you're still not the boss type.'

There was the sound of a TV being turned on and suddenly Tom's heart leapt when he heard a voice he knew: Vince Winter.

Good evening, Vince said, *it's a perfect night for baseball.* As his deep voice went on, describing the scene at Exhibition Stadium, Tom was filled with an aching loneliness. Would he ever see Vince again?

If only he could escape!

Fantastic! Vince exclaimed. *What a catch by Dexter Valentine!*

The memory of the happy scene on the Valentines' balcony only a few hours before made Tom even more determined to escape. He still had no idea why he had been kidnapped, but he knew he had to

34

seize the chance provided by the baseball broadcast to get free.

Carefully, he examined the room. There was only the one locked door and the window had been nailed shut. He was trapped.

Or was he? Tom looked at a small wooden chair in the corner, and considered his chances. Then he went quickly over to the chair, picked it up and approached the window.

Using all his strength, Tom swung the chair. With a terrible *crash* the glass splintered; startled cries came from the hallway as Tom knocked away loose bits of glass and quickly climbed through the frame.

As his feet touched the ground, a light went on inside the room behind him and Tom was caught in its glare. He plunged into the darkness, almost collided with a tree, then stumbled on into the bushes.

'Come back!' the blacksmith shouted.

Tom fought a path through the bushes until he reached the rocky side of a hill. He scrambled on, pausing occasionally to listen for sounds that he was being pursued.

Apart from the cold stars above, he was surrounded by darkness. There was no sound except the shrill calling of frogs, and Tom knew he'd escaped safely.

For a moment this thrilled him, but then a gust of wind chilled his face and he looked around. Where could he possibly go in the endless, empty darkness?

5

For a while Tom blundered on.

He climbed another hill, hoping for signs of civilization, but found only darkness. He thought he heard traffic, but he was mistaken.

Finally, shivering with cold and fear, he sat under a tree and hugged his body for warmth. It was hopeless to go any further until dawn.

Throughout the long night he dreamed of fireplaces with roaring flames, and of a luxurious hot bath in which he was soaking, while diamonds sparkled nearby. He woke often, his body stiff, then returned to his dreams.

Birdsong came before morning. Tom lay listening to it as the dawn's faint light revealed a white fungus clinging to a dead stump, then the bare branches of a tree overhead.

At last the sun came up, and he saw a forest of barren trees, wrapped in mist. Standing, he stretched his cramped muscles. If he went toward the sun, which was glowing feebly behind the thick grey mist, he would avoid walking in circles and must eventually find help.

Twigs snapped underfoot as Tom started down the hill. Suddenly he stopped. Was that a car he'd heard? No, it was just the wind gusting through bare branches.

At the foot of the hill, Tom came to a dirt road. A hawk rose from the ditch with a snake in its talons; briefly it was silhouetted against the cold grey sky before it disappeared.

'Wow!' Tom whispered. 'What a sight.'

Hoping that the hawk was a lucky sign, he walked in the direction it had gone. The road was surrounded by the browns and greys of the forest; although it was April, the air was far too cold for the trees to be budding yet.

Despite his stiff muscles, and the hunger which ached inside his stomach, Tom felt cheerful as he followed the road up a hill. People must live around here somewhere, and soon he'd be safe.

At the top of the hill Tom stopped dead in his tracks. Parked on the road ahead was the station wagon used by his kidnappers the previous evening.

Dropping to the ground, he studied the station wagon. It was parked near a phone booth, in which Tom could see the blacksmith gesturing with his hand while talking to someone on the phone. He hung up and went to speak to a man leaning against the station wagon; with a jolt of surprise, Tom realized that this was the chauffeur from Casa Loma.

Both men wore red-checked wool coats, and their breath came out in puffs as they talked. Then they split up, the chauffeur going into the woods, while the blacksmith entered the trees on the other side of the road.

When they were lost from sight, Tom hurried toward the phone booth to call the police. He was so cold and tired that he needed help soon, and he was sure the men would take time searching the woods.

Tom glanced at the rear of the station wagon, then reached for the phone. His hand was shaking so much he could hardly hold it.

'Please answer!' he whispered, listening to the phone ring in some distant office. 'Please!'

As he waited, Tom looked again at the station wagon. On the driver's side there was a small rear-view mirror, which reflected the eyes of someone inside. This person seemed half asleep, but any second the eyes would surely open and spot him.

The ringing stopped, and a voice answered. 'Police headquarters.'

'Uh.' Tom stared at the two eyes, which were all he could see of the driver's face. He knew those eyes, but where from? 'Hello, police?' he whispered.

'Would you speak up? The line's so bad, I can hardly hear you.'

'I need help,' Tom said, as loud as he dared.

'Please make your call again. I can't hear anything.'

'Listen . . .'

As the line went dead, the eyes spotted Tom. For a moment they stared in shock, then the station wagon's horn blared; the still morning air was shattered by the sound as Tom stumbled out of the booth and started running.

He knew at any second he'd hear the sound of the car door opening and the driver running after him. The thought forced Tom's aching legs to carry him up the road and into the woods.

For a second he paused. The horn was still blaring, which must mean the driver had chosen to signal for the others instead of giving chase. This was a real break, and Tom used it to plunge deeper into the trees.

At last the horn stopped. Tom reached a stony outcrop and looked down into a deep river, swollen with the spring flood. Crawling behind a rock, he tried desperately to think; the men would know the direction he'd gone, and would soon be coming this way. How could he save himself?

A minute later, Tom had a plan. Putting his shoulder against the largest boulder on the out-cropping, he worked it loose. Then he waited until he could hear the sound of feet crashing through the trees.

Tom pushed with all his strength against the boulder. It hesitated, then rolled over the edge of the outcropping, and plunged down toward the swirling black water below. As it fell, Tom cupped his mouth and screamed, 'No!'

The boulder hit the water with a tremendous splash. Tom scrambled along the outcropping to the shelter of a big tree and dropped behind it, shaking.

'That was the kid!' the blacksmith shouted from

somewhere in the trees. 'He must have fallen in the river!'

'Perfect! Let's go and fish him out.'

The chattering of an angry squirrel announced the approach of the men. Tom held his breath.

'Look at that water!' the blacksmith said. 'He didn't have a chance. I can't even see his body.'

'It must be way downstream already. We'd better get out of here.'

They hurried away, but Tom remained in hiding long after he'd heard the station wagon drive off. It was possible the men suspected a trick, and one had remained behind to watch the woods.

Finally hunger and cold forced Tom to move. He worked his way cautiously back toward the road until he could see the phone booth; after checking that the coast was clear he stepped out.

There was no sign of the men. He hurried to the phone booth, desperate now to contact the police. The phone was dead.

'They've cut the line! I don't believe it.'

Tom stared at the useless instrument, feeling his spirits ebb away. What could he do now? Slumped against the booth, he stared at the grey mist and barren trees.

The dead phone meant the men didn't fully believe he had fallen in the river and drowned, and they might return at any moment. Tom knew he must move on, yet he couldn't find the energy; it didn't seem worth the effort.

A porcupine came out of the woods and lumbered slowly across the road. Tom looked at its sharp quills and smiled at the porcupine's rolling gait. It looked like a near-sighted gentleman, bound for the Millionaires' Club.

One more try. Tom started along the road on feet that now felt like blocks of ice, blowing on his pinched fingers as he went. A tiny bird swept out of a pine tree and swooped round Tom's head in an attempt to defend its nest. Tom trudged wearily on.

As he rounded the next bend, Tom saw a lake and in the distance, along the shoreline there was a large cabin with a twist of smoke rising from its stone chimney.

'People! At last, real people!'

At this moment, as if in a final effort to break him, rain began to fall. Big drops splattered on Tom's face as he left the road to follow the shoreline round to the distant cabin.

'Don't be a mirage!' he said. 'Please stay where you are.'

A flock of small birds was exploring the wild grass along the shoreline. A blue heron took off from the shore, rising gracefully over the still lake, where the falling raindrops were forming hundreds of perfect circles.

Reaching the cabin, Tom noticed a ribbon of road winding out of the woods to a garage with a moss-covered roof. The road was littered with dead branches from winter storms, giving it a deserted appearance, but fresh footsteps and two long tracks leading from the garage to the cabin meant it was inhabited.

Tom thumped on the cabin's side door with his hand, and called for help. When there was no reply, he hit the door again, feeling his numb hand throb with pain.

'Who's there?' a voice shouted from inside.

The thrill of hearing a voice, and knowing he was safe at last, fed energy into Tom's system. 'Help me!' he shouted.

'I'll be right with you.'

Tom stepped back from the door. Moving about to keep his blood circulating, he walked round to the front of the cabin.

One of the windows was smashed.

Tom stared at the scattered glass, refusing to believe his eyes. Then he heard the cabin door open, and his heart jumped as he turned to see the blacksmith.

6

The man glared at Tom.

'So you tricked us, boy.'

'No,' Tom whispered. 'Please, leave me alone.'

The blacksmith walked forward, his huge hands clenched. Tom stared past him at the woods, realizing he couldn't reach their safety, then he ran toward the lake.

A pier stood over the water; Tom's feet slipped on its wet surface as he ran to the end. There were no boats. He looked at the rain falling on the black water. Knowing it was foolish to even consider swimming, he turned round to face the blacksmith, who was close behind him. The pier was narrow, and there was no hope of darting past him to safety.

'Get away from me,' Tom begged, backing away.

He took another step back, but his foot found only

emptiness. With a cry he fell backwards into the lake and freezing water closed over his head.

Tom struggled to the surface and swam toward a ladder on the pier. With the last of his energy he climbed it, and collapsed at the blacksmith's feet.

The man lifted Tom in his powerful arms. 'Enjoy your swim?'

'Leave me alone,' Tom gasped. 'I'm . . . I'm . . .'

'Where are the diamonds?'

Tom stared at him, for a moment unable to understand.

'Tell me where the diamonds are hidden.'

'I . . .' Tom paused, trying to control his chattering teeth. 'I . . . don't . . . know.'

The blacksmith stepped toward the water. 'In you go.'

'No! I'll tell.'

'You've got two seconds, then you're back in the lake.'

'They're . . .' Tom gasped for breath. 'They're in . . . Sir Nigel's . . . shower.'

The blacksmith's mean eyes studied Tom's face, and for a terrible moment the man seemed ready to throw him into the lake again. Then he nodded.

'I think you're telling the truth.'

'I . . . am!'

'For your sake, I hope so.'

Carrying Tom in his powerful arms, the blacksmith returned to the cabin, and soon Tom was lying in a hot bath, feeling it draw the chill from his bones.

Later he sat at a rough-cut wooden table, watching the blacksmith throw chunks of log into a pot-bellied stove. Despite what had happened, Tom was too hungry to feel anything but thankful as the man dropped bacon, and then eggs, into a sizzling frying pan.

His clothes were drying beside the stove. The blacksmith had provided an old dressing-gown; Tom pulled it tighter round himself, working up courage.

'Where's the chauffeur?'

No reply.

'And the driver of the station wagon. I've forgotten the name just now, but you know who I mean. I don't see them around.'

The blacksmith scooped the bacon and eggs on to a tin plate, and dropped it in front of Tom on the table. He looked at Tom for a moment without saying anything, then he returned to the stove.

The first taste of food was marvellous. 'This is great! May I have some toast, please?' Tom swallowed quickly, too hungry to savour the food. 'You three will be arrested for kidnapping. Doesn't that worry you?'

The blacksmith poured coffee from a blackened pot, and downed it in one long swallow. He hadn't spoken a word since leaving the pier; his silence was a perfect armour against Tom's probing questions.

'You're a terrific cook,' Tom said, trying to get somewhere by soft-talking the man. 'You should be a chef, not a criminal. You don't seem the outlaw type to me.'

The blacksmith glanced at Tom, and something flickered in his eyes.

'It's time for you to get some sleep,' he said gruffly. 'I'm tired of your questions.'

Tom fell silent, afraid he had pushed the man too far. He followed him to a room with a bare mattress and a sleeping bag. Crawling into it, he burrowed a warm place and closed his eyes. With vivid clarity, he re-enacted in his mind the scene as he had approached the cabin. He recalled the rising smoke, the blue heron, the dead branches on the road, but he was sure the memory held something important that he'd overlooked. He'd almost figured it out when he fell asleep.

Some time later, the blacksmith shook him awake. Barely able to focus his eyes, Tom dragged on his clothes and was taken outside, where the station wagon was waiting.

He dropped into the rear seat and wearily closed his eyes. Then suddenly, without warning, he was blindfolded and shoved on to the floor by the black-smith.

'Oh no! Hey, it's horrible down here. Please let me up.'

Silence.

'Are you afraid I'll recognize the person who drives this thing? I promise not to look.'

His pleas were in vain. The station wagon was soon under way, and Tom remained on the floor. Again he slept, but fitfully.

Tom was awakened by the squeal of brakes. Rough hands seized him, and he was pushed out of the station wagon. He tore off his blindfold, hoping to get the station wagon's number or a glimpse of the driver, but it had already disappeared among the trees.

Tom kicked the dirt in annoyance, then looked around the small park in which he stood. There was no sign of people, so he hurried toward the sound of traffic to find help.

By the time he reached the street, however, he'd had time to think. It would be better if he could find the diamonds before he contacted the police. He stopped a woman and asked her where he could catch the streetcar to Casa Loma.

'Streetcars don't go near there.' She pointed at a TTC sign. 'Take the subway to the Dupont stop.'

'Thanks.'

It was a long ride and Tom tried to curb his impatience by sitting in the front car, where he watched blue and red signal lights flash past as the train raced through the twisting tunnels. At Dupont he climbed to the street and hurried toward Casa Loma; in just a few more minutes he could tell Uncle Henry about the shower and help him to take it apart. He just hoped that the crooks hadn't got there first.

There was no Smythe to open the castle's front door, but Tom had too much on his mind to wonder where the man was. He rushed from room to room in desperation until he finally spotted Liz and his uncle in the conservatory.

Swinging open a door, he hurried in. 'I'm back!'

Liz glanced his way. 'Hi, Tom.'

Uncle Henry smiled. 'Enjoy your swim? I hope the water wasn't too cold.'

Staggered, Tom stared at the two. Surely they weren't involved in his kidnapping? His shock then turned to amazement as they returned to their conversation.

'Hey!' he said. 'I'm safe!'

Liz looked his way, puzzled. 'Have you been nibbling mouldy crackers again? Of course you're safe.'

'Well, don't you care?'

'You're spoiling our fun, Tom. We're trying to act nonchalant, so you don't know we've got a secret.'

'But don't you realize I was *kidnapped* yesterday?'

'Sure you were,' Liz said. 'And the cow jumped over the moon.'

'Listen to me! I was grabbed by the Casa Loma blacksmith and chauffeur, taken to some cabin, chased through the woods, I don't know what all happened. Then I come home to *this*! Where do you think I've been all this time?'

Uncle Henry went to a chair and sat down. 'The chauffeur's wife phoned last night, Tom. She said they'd invited you to stay overnight, and you were delighted because their apartment building has a swimming pool.'

'Lies!'

'So I gather. Then what actually happened?'

Tom told the full story, including his theory about the diamonds' hiding-place. Liz and Uncle Henry glanced at each other when he mentioned the jewels, but remained silent.

Uncle Henry polished his glasses thoughtfully and said, 'This is serious, Tom. We must contact the police.'

'What's the use? Both men will have disappeared by now, if they've any sense. Besides, I've got no proof against them, and I haven't got clue one where that cabin is located.'

'What about the third person?'

'All I had was a glimpse of the driver's eyes in the rear-view mirror. Hey, I'm starving. Do you think Irene would fetch me a snack?'

'Irene's left us.'

'Irene? I don't believe it!'

Uncle Henry shook his head unhappily. 'I'm afraid it's true, Tom. One of the servants has just told me. Apparently Irene suddenly announced she was quitting, and walked out of the door without saying good-bye.'

'What a rotten thing to do.'

'Yes, I don't understand it after she's been so friendly to us all.'

'Do you think she quit because of Smythe?'

'Who knows? Anyway, we've seen the last of him. He's quit too.'

'*What!*'

'He also left today, without an explanation.' Uncle Henry tried to smile. 'It seems I'm not a very successful employer. The staff of Casa Loma is in tatters, and I've only been here three days.'

'Surely no one else has gone?'

'A couple of others resigned, and Tia had to go home yesterday. She's got the flu. I can't get replacements until she's back, and can conduct interviews.'

His face was so bleak that Tom almost smiled. Running a castle wasn't proving to be much fun; any more staff losses and Uncle Henry's entire day would be spent cleaning the fifteen bathrooms and replacing Casa Loma's five thousand light bulbs.

'Cheer up, Unc. Let's go and check out Sir Nigel's shower for the diamonds.'

'I almost forgot!' Uncle Henry smiled at Liz. 'We haven't told Tom our secret.'

They lead Tom down Peacock Alley to the door of Sir Nigel's study. Uncle Henry unlocked it, waved the others inside, then secured the door against intruders.

Puzzled, Tom looked at the oil paintings of ancient gentlemen in wigs, then at the chandelier and the mahogany walls. He wondered what the big secret could be. Liz went to stand by the marble fireplace, while Uncle Henry sat at the desk and ran his fingers over one of its carved eagles.

'Look at this, Tom.' Uncle Henry opened a drawer and slid aside a section at the back, then took a small velvet box from hiding.

Tom shivered with excitement as the box was put in his hands. He lifted the top, and his eyes were dazzled by the white fire inside.

'The diamonds! I don't believe it!'

7

For a few minutes, Tom could only stare.

'But . . .? How . . .?'

'It was simple.' Uncle Henry put his feet up on
the desk, and fiddled happily with an old quill pen.
'Want to know how we found them?'

'Of course!'

'Well, we just came to this desk and opened the
false drawer.' He smiled. 'Of course, we had a little
help before that.'

'What was it?'

'Someone phoned this morning, Tom. He wouldn't
give his name, but he told me exactly where to find
the diamonds. Vince Winter was here having coffee,
so the two of us plus Liz and Smythe dashed to the
study . . . and you know the rest.'

'Brother! After all my running around in the

woods, and a ducking in the lake, I finally get set to dig out the diamonds and you've beaten me to it!'

'Sorry, Tom. We should have waited before opening the desk.'

'No, no.' Tom tried to smile, but he still felt disappointed. 'I'm glad you found the diamonds. Too bad Sir Nigel wasn't in the desk too.'

'I agree. Then he could have this crazy castle back.' Uncle Henry looked at his watch. 'I'd better go and arrange for some afternoon tea. The cook may forget, now there isn't a butler to keep things moving.'

When he'd left, Liz smiled. 'We were in the kitchen this morning. The stove is actually big enough to roast a whole ox.'

'Is that right, eh?'

'You sound blue, Tom.'

'Yeah.' He put his finger in the velvet box, and pushed around the glittering jewels. 'Shouldn't these be somewhere safe?'

'Uncle Henry is leaving them hidden in the desk overnight. Tomorrow they're going into a safety-deposit box at the bank.'

'Will they be O.K. here?'

'Sure. The rest of the servants will have resigned by six o'clock, so there'll be no one left to steal them.'

Tom watched Liz put away the velvet box, then close the secret section. He had to admit the apparently empty drawer made a clever hiding-place.

'There's still a lot of unanswered questions, Liz. For example, the clue Sir Nigel gave Tia doesn't fit with a desk drawer, although he could have been just teasing her, I guess.' Tom walked over to the marble fireplace. 'There's also that weird thing I overheard the blacksmith say when I was being held prisoner at the cabin.'

'What was that?'

'He said something about the study having a latch instead of a button. I thought maybe he was talking about this study, since this is where Sir Nigel disappeared.'

'Well, it beats me.'

'And me.'

Still feeling chilly from his night in the open, Tom decided to take a shower. Leaving Liz sitting in the study, staring at a scrap of paper on which she'd written *study-latch-button*, he found Uncle Henry and received permission to try Sir Nigel's shower again.

To his delight, it decided to co-operate this time, and thin needles of hot water hissed from the rails until Tom had nearly drained the castle's boiler. Lazily he dried himself. He was sorry he hadn't been correct about the shower concealing the diamonds, but he was glad they were safe.

Returning to the study, he found Liz with her feet on the desk and a wrap-around grin on her face.

'I deserve a large medal,' she said.

'What happened?'

'Tell me again about Irene opening the secret panel in Sir Nigel's bedroom?'

'Well, she just pushed a button under the mantel, and the panel swung open.'

'Don't you get it? In the bedroom a button, in the study . . .'

'A latch!'

'Watch this.' Liz crossed the luxurious rug to the fireplace and reached under the mantel.

Silently, a mahogany panel swung open in the wall.

'Good grief!' Tom went forward to gaze at the narrow stairs leading down into darkness. 'Well done, Liz.'

'Thanks,' she said, smiling.

'Where do they go?'

'Don't ask me. I'm too chicken to go down there alone.'

Gingerly, Tom put his foot on the top stair. It creaked, and he stepped quickly back.

Liz smiled. 'Come on, let's try them together.'

Tom followed her into the darkness. The narrow wooden stairs spiralled down, and the light of the study was left behind. The air was musty and freezing cold.

'Concrete,' Liz whispered. 'I think we've reached a tunnel.'

'There must be a light.'

'Let's search.'

Tom stretched out his hand, and his fingers touched cold cement. He felt his way along it, but found nothing.

'Want to turn back?' Liz whispered.

'No way. Let's see where this leads.'

Liz's face was a dim white smudge in the darkness; she started along the tunnel, and disappeared.

'Slow down!' Tom said. 'I can't see anything.'

'Keep your hand on the wall as a guide.'

'What if there's a pit ahead?'

'Nice thing to say, when I'm going first.'

'I'm sorry, Liz, I didn't mean that. Actually, this tunnel leads to the lair of the Huge Hairy Spider of Casa Loma. Apparently it needs a big supply of girls as bubble gum.'

Liz laughed weakly, then they both fell silent. The only sound came from their hesitant footsteps and nervous breathing as, slowly and carefully, they worked their way forward through the cold black air.

'This is crazy,' Tom whispered after a while. 'We could walk for ever.'

'The tunnel must lead somewhere. It just seems long because we're moving so slowly.'

'Listen! Is that water?'

'I think it's only a drip. Or else it's the Huge Hairy Spider, drooling.'

'Two more minutes, then we turn back.'

'O.K.'

They moved on, and Tom's nerves were on edge as he pictured pits and spiders waiting in the darkness. He was beginning to wish the secret panel had remained a secret when an urgent *hssst!* came from Liz.

'Stairs!' she whispered. 'Leading up.'

'I wonder where to?'

'We'll soon know.'

The wooden stairs creaked underfoot, as they climbed slowly up them. At the top, there was a scrabbling sound as Liz's hands searched the wall for an opening of some sort. Suddenly there was a click, and pale light seeped through a narrow crack.

'We're in the stables!'

'Are you sure?'

The crack grew wider as Liz pushed open a panel in the wall, and beyond Tom could see the narrow passage that led to the horse stalls.

'So that's it! This is how they got Sir Nigel and Hatfield out of the study.'

Liz nodded. 'The blacksmith probably did the dirty work. He must have knocked Sir Nigel over the head, then hauled him through the tunnel to the stables. Ditto with Hatfield.'

'But then what happened to Sir Nigel?'

'Listen!'

From somewhere in the stables came a muffled thudding. Tom grew tense as he followed Liz along the passage toward the sound; what if the blacksmith was waiting with one of his mallets?

They turned a corner and found themselves in the horse stalls. The thudding was much louder.

'It's coming from that end stall.'

They hurried across the tiled floor and stopped in front of a padlocked door. Looking round Tom found a pair of the blacksmith's tongs, and used them to force the padlock off.

Liz gave the door a quick shove and, with a squeal of metal, it swung open to reveal a small cot.

Lying on it was Sir Nigel Brampton.

His face was flushed from the effort of kicking the wall, and his eyes goggled as he tried to speak through the gag over his mouth. '*Mmmmmph!*' he said then gestured with his bound hands.

'It's O.K.!' Tom said. 'We'll get you untied.'

As he bent over the knots, Sir Nigel continued to

make anxious sounds. The moment Liz removed his gag, Sir Nigel burst out,

'The diamonds! Are they safe?'

'They sure are.' Liz smiled. 'And now you're safe, too.'

'The jewels . . . are you positive?'

'We've just been looking at them. Now try to relax, Sir Nigel. Tom's almost got those knots undone.'

'Thank goodness my diamonds are safe. Those crooks tried everything possible to make me reveal where they were hidden, but I refused!'

'That's great.'

As Tom released the final knot, Sir Nigel sat up on the cot. He smoothed the white hair which fringed his bald head, then smiled. 'Thank you both for rescuing me. I've kicked and kicked that wall, but no one ever heard.' He tried to stand, then sank back with a groan.

'You're not well,' Liz said anxiously. 'We'd better get help.'

'Nonsense. I'm fine.' Sir Nigel staggered up, but again he collapsed. 'Perhaps you're right. I do need assistance.'

Tom went to the door. 'Wait here. I'll ask Uncle Henry to phone for an ambulance.' Hurrying through the stables, he noticed the forge and suddenly realized why the blacksmith was always pounding cold horseshoes. Obviously it was to drown out Sir Nigel's efforts to attract attention when anyone came to the stables.

A second puzzle was answered when Tom remembered the chauffeur with the tray of food. He must have brought it through the tunnel for Sir Nigel, which explained his dry clothes.

The jigsaw was slowly falling together, and yet Tom didn't feel elated. Somehow, he sensed that the mystery and danger were far from over.

8

The big man swung hard.

There was a loud *crack* as his bat hit the ball, and he broke into a run. Cries of alarm turned suddenly to cheers as Dexter Valentine dived for the ball, then threw it with lightning speed to first base.

'You're out!' the umpire shouted, as the batter reached the base a split-second after the ball.

Thousands of cheering voices filled the night, and another Blue Jays baseball game was under way.

'Did you see that play?' Tom exclaimed. 'That was my buddy, Dexter!'

Liz laughed. 'Your buddy? You didn't know the guy two days ago.'

'I make friends fast.' Smiling, Tom turned to look at Vince Winter inside a nearby glass-walled broadcast booth. Vince had loosened his tie, and was excitedly describing Dexter's play; although the booth was sound-proofed, it was clear that Vince's words were filled with awe.

A cold wind came off nearby Lake Ontario, slicing through Tom's clothes. He shivered, and looked longingly at a man who was carrying a steaming container through the crowd. 'Hot dogs!' the man cried. 'Get your giant red-hots here!'

'You hungry, Liz?'

She nodded. 'I'm going for a Salty Pretzel. Can I get you a hot cat?'

'You bet!'

Tom leaned against the railing which separated the broadcast area from the crowd, and returned to watching the action on the stadium's ultra-green artificial turf.

Dexter was first up for the Blue Jays. He let two strikes past, then sent the ball flashing into left field for a clean single. The crowd erupted in cheers, and Tom danced around the broadcast area. Just then, Liz returned with the food.

'Why the thanksgiving? Is the game over?'

'Funny, funny. Dexter just happens to be a hero, yet again.'

'I'm frozen solid.' Leaning over the railing, Liz pointed at a man whose head was hidden inside a knitted toque reading *Go Jays Go*. 'I'd love one of those. It would be a great souvenir of Toronto.'

The next pitch was fouled off into the crowd, and there was generous applause for the girl who proudly held up the ball after a mad scramble among the fans.

'That's the souvenir I'd like,' Tom said. 'Or even a broken bat.'

Seconds later, as the pitcher unleashed a knuckle-ball, Dexter broke for second base. The crowd rose, screaming, as the throw to second seemed to have Dexter trapped, but with a burst of speed he slid to safety under the tag. The cheering continued as he brushed the dirt off his uniform, then grinned.

'Fantastic!' Liz said. 'Your buddy puts on a great show.'

'I predict he'll score the first run.'

When the batter then rattled a double off the wall, and Dexter crossed home plate to put Toronto in the lead, Tom turned to Liz with a bow. 'Does my accurate prediction earn me the rest of your pretzel?'

'No way, Mac!'

The Milwaukee pitcher was in deep trouble, and Tom felt sorry for the man as the team's manager walked slowly to the mound, frowning. They spoke briefly, then the unhappy pitcher handed over the ball and started toward the dug-out.

'He's heading for the showers. Maybe he'll get lucky and find some diamonds there!'

On a huge screen at one end of the stadium, the pitcher was seen trudging woefully across the field. As this image froze and was replaced by a dog-food commercial, Tom remembered Sir Nigel's clue to Tia about where he'd hidden the diamonds. The clue couldn't possibly have referred to the desk drawer, and again Tom felt uneasy.

'Why am I nervous about the diamonds?'

'Because it was all so simple. One anonymous phone call, and suddenly the mystery is solved.' Liz looked thoughtfully at the cold darkness beyond the stadium, where a winking neon sign advertised a TV station. 'Something about the discovery of the diamonds smells like a very old egg.'

'I wish we knew what.'

The new Milwaukee pitcher quickly got his team out of trouble, and Toronto clung to its one-run lead as the fast-paced action continued. During the seventh-inning stretch, while the fans stood to sing 'Take me out to the ball game', Vince joined Tom and Liz.

'Having fun?'

'You bet!' Tom smiled. 'Can't you arrange for Dexter to foul one up here, so we'll have a souvenir?'

'Although I've worked many miracles, Tom, that one could be difficult. However, I do believe you'll be leaving with a souvenir.'

'Wow! What is it?'

'Patience, patience.'

Liz turned from the railing, where she'd been staring at the crowd. 'May I use your binoculars, Vince?'

'Help yourself. They're in the booth.'

Liz returned with the binoculars and soon had them trained on the crowd huddled under blankets and shaggy coats.

'You know something?' she said at last. 'I'm sure that's Smythe, the old butler, down there.'

'What?' Vince exclaimed. 'Let me look.'

Seizing the binoculars, he carefully studied the man Liz had pointed out. Then he smiled. 'You're wrong, Liz. His nose is a different shape.'

'What about that hacked-up chin?'

'Some other guy with a dull razor blade. Not

everyone is wise enough to buy the electric shavers I advertise on TV.'

Liz took the binoculars again. 'That *is* Smythe. I noticed him a while ago, because he kept looking up here. I wonder what's going on?'

Vince laughed. 'The only action is in your imagination, Liz.'

Vince returned to the booth and Tom took the binoculars. But the man must have become aware of their scrutiny, and Tom saw only his back as he hurried toward an exit.

'Why would Smythe be here? I remember at breakfast on Monday he said only kooks like pro sports.'

'Maybe working at Casa Loma snapped his mainspring, and now he's roaming around like a dangerous madman. Was that foam I saw, dripping from his teeth?'

Tom laughed uneasily.

With a roar, the crowd rose to its feet. A Blue Jays slugger had connected solidly, and the ball was high in the air, gleaming against the black sky. Tracing an arc through the night, it landed beyond the wall for a home run.

'I don't believe it!' Tom released a war whoop, and pounded his hands together. 'What a hit!'

The Blue Jays left their dug-out to congratulate the latest hero, and the crowd applauded for several minutes. Then they settled back anxiously, wondering if Milwaukee would stage a come-back.

By the time the game was over, Tom's fingernails were a mess and the Blue Jays had a 2–0 win. After studying the remains of the money he'd saved for his holiday, Tom decided he could afford three hot dogs as a celebration and set off for the snack bar.

He kept a watchful eye out, but there was no sign of Smythe. Returning to the broadcast booth, Tom gave hot dogs to Liz and Vince, then knocked off his own in a few bites, dribbling ketchup and mustard and onions as he ate.

'Excuse my brother,' Liz said. 'We have to hose him down after most meals.'

Vince laughed. 'You two interested in meeting the Blue Jays? I'm just about to do some interviews.'

'For sure!'

Deep inside the stadium, happy talk and laughter came from the Blue Jays' dressing-room. Just past it, Vince led the way inside a small room where a TV camera was set up ready for his interviews with various players.

The last to be interviewed was Dexter Valentine, and afterwards Tom proudly introduced Liz to him. Vince then asked Dexter to join him in the hallway.

When the two men returned, Dexter was carrying a large carton which Vince had brought down with him from the broadcast booth.

'Liz and Tom,' Dexter said, sounding rather self-conscious and strained, 'I understand you rescued Sir Nigel today?'

'Sort of, I guess,' Liz said, suddenly self-conscious herself. 'We just looked in the right place.'

'I've been asked to present you both with a souvenir, to mark his rescue.'

'Thanks!'

Tom and Liz smiled at Dexter and then at Vince, who waved his hand. 'You deserve it, kids.'

Dexter opened the carton to reveal two satin team-jackets with thick crests reading *Toronto Blue Jays*, and baseball caps with crests. Tom and Liz were delighted, and immediately put them on.

'You look good!' Vince said. 'Let me get a picture of you with Dexter.'

The camera flashed, then Dexter left to change. Vince smiled at Tom and Liz. 'You two feel like a day at Niagara Falls?'

'You bet!'

'I'm going down there to interview a retired tennis pro. Do you think your uncle would let you go along as my guests?'

'He'd better!'

'Then let's drive up to the castle. You can collect your toothbrushes, and we'll leave tonight to get an early start in the morning on the sights.'

Uncle Henry gave permission for the journey, but seemed depressed about something. They left him slumped in front of the fireplace waiting for Sir Nigel, who had insisted on being discharged from hospital and was expected at any minute.

'I wonder what's wrong?' Tom said, as they walked towards Vince's sports car. 'Do you think he's blue because he won't be taking over the castle?'

Liz shook her head. 'No, something else is bothering Unc.'

'Maybe it's the diamonds. There's something weird about them.'

9

Rocking and bucking, the little boat headed into the heart of Horseshoe Falls.

From high above, emerald-green water plunged down with great force on the rocks, forming a steaming white spray.

'This is fantastic!' Tom shouted above the thundering roar of the Falls.

'This is insane!' Liz added, laughing as her face was lashed by needles of spray. 'I'm drowning!'

Wrapped in black rain-slickers, they stood with Vince in the bow of the *Maid of the Mist* as it fought the seething green water to venture deeper toward the Falls. Tom could now see nothing except the white spray which stung his face until he was blinded. He was worried that the captain had taken them too far in and the boat would be crushed to pieces by the terrible fury of the Falls.

But at that moment, as if sensing Tom's alarm, the captain put the boat into reverse and the *Maid of the Mist* slipped slowly out of the spray. Licking water off his lips, Tom grinned.

'Too bad the captain chickened out. I was hoping we'd plough right through the Falls, and see what it's like behind them.'

Liz smiled. 'Say that again, with a straight face.'

Vince pulled back the hood of his slicker, then shook water out of his wavy brown hair. 'Would you really like to go behind the Falls? We've got a little extra time.'

Tom hesitated, knowing his bluff had been called. 'Uh, well . . .'

Liz grinned.

'Sure!' Tom said. 'Let's go.'

'O.K.' Vince pointed up to the top of the Falls, where a crowd of people were watching the *Maid of the Mist*. 'You see that building on top of the cliff?'

'Yup.'

'That's called Table Rock House. From there, elevators take tourists deep inside the rock to tunnels which lead to openings behind the Falls.'

'Is it safe?'

'Let's hope so!'

The boat swung around, and started toward its dock. Tom watched gulls dipping and soaring in the air currents caused by the cascading Falls. A fine mist drifted over the gorge's green waters, and the air smelled wonderfully fresh.

'What a day! The best of my life.'

Vince laughed. 'The excitement isn't over yet.'

After they'd docked, and returned the rain-slickers, Vince and Liz paused at mirrors provided by the company to comb their damp hair. Tom ran a quick hand through his hair, then put on the Blue Jays cap and adjusted his team-jacket, anxious to start the next part of the adventure.

They took an incline-railway car to the top of the gorge where Vince had left his sports car.

'Over there is Rainbow Bridge,' he said, pointing. 'It crosses to the American side of the Falls.'

'You mean that's the USA, just across the gorge?'

'That's right. We'll cross the bridge and look at the Falls from the American viewpoint after we've visited those tunnels.'

'*If* we survive the tunnels,' Tom said, attempting a laugh.

A short while later, they were walking toward Table Rock House when Liz suddenly pointed to a newspaper rack. 'Hey, look at that!'

Under a photograph of Sir Nigel, a huge black headline read: BORDER ALERT FOR GEMS. Liz seized a paper and quickly scanned the article.

'That explains everything!'

'What's it say, Liz?'

She looked up from the paper, her eyes shining with excitement. 'Those so-called diamonds we found at Casa Loma were fakes! They were cheap imitations made from quartz. The police figure the real diamonds have been taken from the castle.'

'Why the border alert?'

'Apparently the police think a couple of Americans are the master-minds behind the theft, and they may be heading for the USA with the diamonds. Travellers are being questioned at border check-points, and some of them are being searched.'

'What a story!' Vince looked envious as he read the article. 'Sometimes I'd love to be in TV news, not sports. Then for sure I'd dig up lots of hot news items like this.'

Tom grabbed the paper and started to read the story. He wondered who the Americans could be. 'Thank goodness Sir Nigel came home last night, and discovered the truth.'

Vince shook his head. 'Look on page two, Tom. It says the police knew the diamonds were fakes long before Sir Nigel got home.'

'But how did they know that?'

No one could suggest an answer. Tom turned to the sports page, hoping to find the photograph Vince had taken of them with Dexter Valentine, but the only picture was captioned *American star thrills Toronto again* and showed Dexter making a sensational diving catch.

Vince looked at his digital watch. 'Come on, people.'

Outside the entrance to Table Rock House, they paused to gaze down into the gorge. Far below, the *Maid of the Mist* was just disappearing into the white spray again; Tom shivered with excitement, as he looked at the massive weight of green water plunging over the nearby cataract.

'Imagine going over those Falls. You'd be knocked to pieces.'

Vince nodded. 'A lot of people have died here. But a few survived.'

'Went over the Falls and lived? Impossible!'

Vince pointed at the wide river which rushed through a series of rapids before dropping over the Falls. 'Back in 1901, a widowed teacher was set adrift on the river inside an oak barrel. She was looking for instant fame and fortune by being the first to survive the plunge.'

'Did she live?'

'Yes, but the only money she made was from selling autographed pictures of herself beside the barrel. She died a pauper. Then some guy went over safely in a barrel, only to die later after slipping on a piece of orange peel.'

Tom stared at the roaring water, finding it hard to believe that such strange events had happened right there. 'I think Mr Stones told our class about some kid surviving the Falls.'

'That's right, a seven-year-old boy was in a boating accident on the river. His life-jacket kept him afloat all through the rapids, and he was so light that he was then thrown straight out over the Falls. He landed beyond the rocks, and was picked up by the *Maid of the Mist*. No damage done, except a couple of cuts.'

Liz looked at a log trapped between two boulders near the lip of the Falls, then stared at the foaming white rapids. 'Imagine boating on such a dangerous river. If I ever do that, please have my head tested.'

Vince laughed. 'You're right, Liz. Although I'm an avid sportsman, a boat ride through the Niagara rapids is one thrill I'm not after.'

'Speaking of thrills, how about those tunnels?'
'Follow me!'

Inside Table Rock House, they were directed to a changing-room which looked like a scene from a science fiction movie. Attendants dressed in yellow prepared the tourists for the tunnels by replacing their shoes with huge gumboots and wrapping each person inside a black rubber rain-slicker and hood. On Vince's suggestion, Tom and Liz kept their Blue Jays caps and team-jackets on under their slickers.

Tom waddled toward the elevator, his feet sliding around inside the gumboots and his head buried under the greasy rubber hood. Smiling, he watched a large group of tourists chattering happily in a foreign language as they posed for pictures in their black gear.

Everyone jammed inside the elevator for the trip down. The noisy conversation continued until the elevator doors opened without warning and the tourists were silenced by the roar of the Falls.

The booming thunder of the water filled the narrow tunnel. A little child belonging to one of the other tourists started to cry. He was picked up and the group shuffled out of the elevator.

'This way!' Vince yelled, pointing along the tunnel.

Tom nodded and smiled, but his heart was beating fast. The deafening noise of the water made him wonder if they should keep away from the plunging Falls. But then he realized that it must be safe, or tourists would not be allowed down here.

'Fabulous, eh?' he shouted to Liz.

She smiled nervously. 'I hope Vince knows what he's doing! I'd hate to fall in.'

'We'll be fine!'

The long tunnel was lined with orange, white and red lights. Tom was again reminded of a scene from a science fiction movie as he looked at the eerie figures of the other tourists, hidden inside their identical black slickers. A person could commit a murder here, and never be identified.

Rounding a corner, he suddenly saw the water.

It fell in a solid sheet of white, roaring down on to the rocks and steaming up in clouds of spray through the narrow tunnel opening. Tom stared at it in fascination.

Finally he backed away, and followed a second tunnel toward another opening. There were yet more tourists here, and he had to wait his turn to approach the flimsy wooden railing which warned *Danger: do not climb over.*

A few people left the railing and came along the tunnel toward Tom, shouting to each other in a foreign language. He smiled at them, then looked at the group still standing by the railings. At that moment, one man turned his head.

It was Smythe.

10

The man returned to studying the plunging water, and was again camouflaged by his hooded slicker. Tom's heart thumped fearfully, and he moved carefully away, hoping he wouldn't be spotted.

Then he turned and hurried back to the other tunnel. 'Vince!' he shouted, going from figure to figure until he found him. 'I just saw Smythe!'

Vince looked stunned. 'Are you certain?'

'Yes! It was him, shaving cuts and all. He's in the other tunnel!'

Vince was silent for a moment. Then he led Tom and Liz away from the other tourists. 'Listen carefully!' he said. 'It's time for the truth. I'm a Mountie, working undercover on the Casa Loma case. Things are getting hot, and I'll need your help, if the crooks aren't going to get away!'

'Wow!' Tom exclaimed. 'Sure thing!'

Liz nodded.

'Good. Now listen, the real reason I'm at Niagara Falls is to watch for Smythe, in case he tries to cross the border with the diamonds. Thanks to your quick eyes, Tom, he's been spotted.'

Tom glowed.

'I can't tackle him alone, in case he's armed and someone gets shot. We'll need to keep him down here, while we go for help.'

Vince quickly outlined his plan, and Tom rushed back to the tunnel where he'd spotted Smythe.

It was jammed with tourists, and Tom's spirits sank as he hurried from figure to figure without finding Smythe. Had he made a get-away? Then suddenly Tom spotted him.

'Smythe! Please help me!' he called.

The man looked shocked, then started to speak, but Tom cut him off.

'Quick, my sister's in terrible danger!'

Tom started to run. He glanced over his shoulder to check Smythe was following, then pushed through the tourists toward the thundering water where Liz stood waiting.

She turned, her face wet with spray, and screamed when she saw Smythe. Her legs buckled, and she collapsed on to a rock beside the thundering Falls.

'Help her!' Tom cried.

Smythe pushed him aside, and bent over Liz. Just then Vince came along the tunnel with two muscular-looking men in slickers.

'That's him!' he yelled, pointing at Smythe. 'You

see, he's tried to push that girl over the side. Grab him!'

Smythe glanced up, puzzled, then gave a startled cry as the men seized his arms and shoved him against the rock wall. Liz scrambled to her feet, and quickly followed Tom along the tunnel; behind them, Smythe shouted angrily but his words were lost in the roar of the water.

Vince joined them at the elevator, his eyes bright. 'Good work! Those men will hold Smythe until we get back with some help.'

As the elevator doors closed on the fury of the water, the silence was a sudden contrast to the noise which had been pounding inside Tom's head. Releasing a deep sigh, he looked at Vince.

'Who's your second suspect?'

'What?'

'The newspaper said that the police suspected that there were two Americans behind the theft.'

'Oh.' Vince paused to shake water out of his hair. 'I'm sorry, but I can't give you that information.'

'Is it someone I know?'

Vince smiled. 'You're a devil, aren't you? O.K., I admit you know the person, but no more questions now. There's no time.'

'Wow!' Tom tapped his foot impatiently as the elevator rose slowly through the rock, then turned to Vince. 'Is it a man or a woman?'

At that moment the elevator reached the top. Vince pushed Tom and Liz out and in to the changing-room to collect their shoes. Soon they were racing across the crowded parking lot to his car. They pulled out of the parking lot at top speed and headed through the streets of the town.

'Where's the police station?' Tom shouted, hanging on tight as they flew around a corner.

'Not far.'

Liz looked at Vince. 'Isn't that Rainbow Bridge straight ahead?'

'That's right! We're crossing to the American side to alert the FBI to increase their border guard. Smythe's partner is almost certainly here too.'

At the middle of the bridge they passed the flags of Canada, the United Nations and the USA. Tom looked beyond them to the distant Horseshoe Falls, then straight down at the swirling waters of the gorge, far below.

'Hopping horntoads! That's a long drop.'

Vince laughed. 'How'd you like to cross this gorge on a tightrope?'

'No thanks! Not for every diamond in the world.'

'The Great Blondin did a lot of tightrope stunts over this gorge.' The car stopped on the bridge, waiting for vehicles ahead to pass through the border check-point. 'He did back-somersaults, rode a bike across, even cooked an omelette out there.'

'Cheese or mushroom?' Liz asked.

Vince laughed, then gestured impatiently. 'What a time to be delayed! Come on, traffic, move!'

'Put on your siren, and pass the others,' Tom suggested.

'This sports car didn't come with a siren.' Vince chewed a fingernail, then relaxed as they moved closer to the check-point. 'It's O.K., kids! We're going to make it safely.'

'Did The Great Blob ever fall?'

'Nope. He came close to it once though, when he carried a man across on his back and the tightrope swayed wildly. But they managed to reach safety.'

Liz shook her head. 'Men are crazy.'

'A woman did stunts, too. She walked the tightrope backwards, then crossed with her head covered by a bag. Another time she had her feet inside peach baskets.'

'What a way to make a buck!'

'You're right, Liz.' Vince smiled happily. 'I'm making lots of bucks, but not by risking my neck.'

They drove toward a row of booths where multicoloured flags flapped in the wind and uniformed officials questioned occupants of the vehicles coming off the bridge.

'I'll do the talking,' Vince said, stopping the car at a booth. Getting out, he had a short conversation with the official, but only his charming laugh could be heard inside the car.

'This is no laughing matter,' Liz said. 'Smythe could have escaped by now.'

'Not with those two big bruisers holding him. But I still wish Vince would hurry!'

Finally Vince got back into the car, and drove to a nearby parking lot. 'They need me inside the customs office. I won't be long. You kids, stay here.'

'Have the officials seen anything of Smythe's partner?'

'Apparently not.'

Vince disappeared inside the customs office. Long moments passed and still he didn't reappear. What could be keeping him? At last they saw him leave the customs building, smiling broadly, and come their way with an official.

'Hop out, kids! You've got some questions to answer.'

Tom gave Liz a puzzled glance as they got out. The official consulted his clipboard, then studied their faces. 'Where were you born?'

'Winnipeg.'

'Bringing any goods into the USA?'

'No, sir.'

'Staying more than twenty-four hours?'

'No.'

After a few more questions, the official gave Vince's car a thorough examination. Then he nodded, and walked away.

'We did it!' Vince exclaimed. 'Let's get going.'

Gunning the engine, Vince took the car out of the parking lot on smoking wheels.

'Is this really the USA?' Tom said, feeling disappointed as he looked at hotels and stores lining the wide streets. 'It's just like Canada.'

Vince smiled. 'Could be, but it looks like home to me.'

'Oh yeah, I forgot. You're from the USA.'

Liz's grip tightened as the sports car swerved around a corner, then she frowned. 'Are you an American, Vince? I didn't know that.'

'Yeah, I'm from good old San-Fran. I think that's the first place I'll visit, now I'm home again.'

'But aren't you going back to Canada?'

'Sure, sure. I'm just talking about the extended holiday I'm planning.'

Leaving the buildings behind, they drove into a

park. The occasional person could be seen walking a dog, but otherwise the park seemed deserted as they followed a road toward a wide body of water.

'Isn't that the Niagara River?'

Vince nodded. 'From here it flows down through the rapids, then drops over the Falls. You see all those trees on the far side of the river? That's Canada.'

Liz glanced at the river, then returned her puzzled gaze to Vince's face. 'A park seems a strange place for the FBI office. Anyway, you sure could have saved time by phoning from the bridge.'

'You're right, Liz.' Vince swung the wheel, and the car pulled to a stop behind a fast-food stand. 'Wait here while I phone. Can I bring you something to eat?'

'A hot dog for me, please!' Tom said.

Liz shook her head. 'Nothing, thanks.'

When Vince was gone, she rubbed her cheek thoughtfully. 'Remember what I said about the discovery of the diamonds smelling like a very old egg? Well, my nose is twitching again.'

'You think there's something strange about this trip?'

Liz nodded.

'Me too. I tell myself that Vince has been good to us, but another voice inside keeps asking a lot of questions. Like, if Vince really is a Mountie, why were we held up for so long by the customs on the bridge?'

'And here's another question: why are we the only customers at this stand? Can the food be that bad?'

'Either that, or it's closed.'

'Then why hasn't Vince come back?'

'Maybe he's decided to swim to the FBI office.'

'Anything seems possible with Vince.' Liz opened the door. 'Let's go and investigate.'

Tom nodded, and they got out. A cold wind was whipping up white-caps on the river, and the bare branches of trees rattled as Tom and Liz cautiously approached the front of the stand and found it locked; a cobwebbed sign inside said, *See you in the summer!* A phone booth stood nearby, but there was no sign of Vince.

'So where is he?'

'In those woods, I think,' Tom said nervously. 'Look.'

Someone was pushing through the thick bushes under the nearby trees. As they parted, and Vince stepped out, Tom caught a glimpse of the roof of a parked vehicle. Then the bushes closed behind Vince, and he smiled.

'Get tired of waiting?'

Liz nodded. 'What's happening, Vince? You're not really a Mountie, are you?'

'Don't you believe me?'

'We want to, Vince. But you're acting so strangely.'

'O.K., my friends, it's time for the truth.' He came forward, grinning, and put his hands on their shoulders. 'You've been more help than you realize.'

'Well, that's good.'

'Let's go for a walk while I explain.'

Still smiling, Vince led the way along a narrow

path through the trees. 'All truth-seekers, follow me!' he exclaimed happily, and tried to click his heels.

Tom gave his sister a worried look. 'He's gone nutty, Liz,' he whispered. 'Let's turn back.'

'I think he's harmless. A bit vain, but hardly dangerous.'

The path ended abruptly. To one side a dirt road curved toward the place in the woods where Tom had noticed the parked vehicle; to the other side was open land sloping down to the river bank. A woman in a wheelchair sat on a small dock, watching the waves lap around the pilings.

As she turned and waved cheerfully, Tom gasped in surprise. 'It's Tia!'

'Hi, there,' she called. 'Why'd you take so long?'

Vince smiled as they approached the dock. 'Tom wanted to have a look behind the Falls, so I took them to Table Rock House. I figured one final treat wouldn't hurt, after all the help they've given us.'

'I approve, Vince. Even young law-breakers deserve some fun.'

Tom stared at Tia, trying to understand what she was saying. Then she reached under the cushion of her wheelchair, and his heart lurched as she produced a small pistol.

'Nobody move,' she said.

I I

For a moment there was only silence.

Then a gull screamed over the river, and Tia chuckled. 'Surprised, kids?'

'But . . . ?'

'What a moment of triumph. I'll relish it for ever.'

Suddenly Tom understood. On the path between the dock and the woods there were two long tracks, identical to those near the cabin where he'd been held prisoner. They were the tracks of Tia's wheelchair.

'So, *you* were the driver of the station wagon!'

Tia nodded, still chuckling. She looked at Vince. 'You tell him what happened, partner.'

Vince smiled. 'Remember refusing to say where you thought the diamonds were hidden? I phoned

Tia and she arranged for the men to grab you on the streetcar. They were told to take you to the cabin and try and find out your theory. A bit crude, perhaps, but it worked.'

'So I was right about the diamonds being hidden in Sir Nigel's shower?'

'Yes. As soon as you'd coughed that up, Tia phoned from the cabin and I raced over to Casa Loma. People were used to my being around the castle, so I just wandered up to Sir Nigel's bathroom and locked the door. In a few minutes the main pipe was off, and I was holding a small metal tube full of diamonds.'

'No wonder the shower stopped working for me. The water must have shifted the tube, and it blocked the main pipe.'

Vince started to speak, but Tia cut him off.

'It was my idea to have some fake diamonds already hidden in Sir Nigel's desk. The old fool had shown me the false drawer some time before.'

'He's not an old fool!' Liz protested. 'He gave you a job, and trusted you. It's terrible how you've treated him.'

Tia's cheeks turned red. 'Be quiet, you.'

'I won't be quiet. You're a thief and you should return the diamonds immediately.'

'But I don't have the diamonds, and neither does Vince.'

'What?'

Tia laughed. 'That's shut you up. Now, as I was saying, once the real diamonds were safely out of Casa Loma, the chauffeur phoned your uncle with the tip to look in Sir Nigel's desk. That discovery gave Vince time to make preparations for the jewels to cross the border.'

'But you've just said you don't have the diamonds.'

'*We* don't have them, but you do.'

'What?'

As Tom and Liz stared at Tia, she broke into delighted laughter. 'It's so marvellous! If you could see your faces!'

Vince laughed too, but only briefly. 'Come on, Tia, we've had enough fun at their expense. Time's a-wasting.'

He stepped toward her, but suddenly she stopped laughing and turned the gun his way. 'I said *nobody* move. That includes you, partner.'

'Are you crazy?'

'No, just greedy.' She smiled. 'I've been thinking, Vince. It's stupid to settle for a half-share, when all the diamonds could be mine.'

'Why, you crook! You double-crosser!'

Vince's face turned dark with fury. He started toward Tia but her finger tightened on the trigger, and he stopped dead.

'That's right, partner. Take it easy, or you'll suffer severe lead-poisoning.' Her eyes flicked toward the water, where a small *Niagara Rentals* motor boat was bobbing beside the dock. 'Get in that thing.'

'Why should I?'

'Because I had it specially delivered, just for your get-away. Soon you'll be across the river in Canada, and you can find a nice tree to hide from the Mounties in.'

'What about the kids?'

'They're staying with me as hostages until I reach safety.'

'Keep the diamonds, Tia, but let Tom and Liz come with me.'

'Not a chance. Now get in that boat.'

Tia waited until Vince was in the boat, then she turned to Liz. 'Take off your jacket.'

'So that's it! I should have known.'

Tia chuckled. 'You're a clever young lady, but not clever enough. Give me the jacket!'

Reluctantly, Liz took off the splendid satin jacket and watched Tia tear at the Blue Jays crest. Finally it came apart, and a shower of diamonds sparkled into her lap.

'Beautiful,' she whispered softly, letting the diamonds run through her fingers. 'What a treasure, and it's all mine.'

'May I have my jacket back?'

'Sure.' Tia pocketed the diamonds, then tossed the jacket back to Liz. 'Now yours, Tom.'

When the diamonds from Tom's crest were safely in her pocket, Tia trained her gun on the motor boat. 'That thing won't go far with a leaky hull, partner, so you'd better get travelling. Otherwise I'll try some target practice.'

'You fink! You couldn't have pulled off this operation without me.'

'Hogwash. I was the brains, and you were just hired help. Now take a ride. My finger is getting itchy.'

Muttering angrily, Vince reached for the starter and the engine rumbled into life. On Tia's instructions, Tom went to release the boat's mooring lines.

'Sorry, kid,' said Vince quietly. 'I didn't like tricking you, but how else could I safely smuggle the jewels?'

'I wish we weren't staying with Tia. I'm scared she'll use that gun.'

'She'd plug me in two seconds, but not a couple of kids.' Vince glanced toward Tia, then dropped his voice even lower. 'Say, good buddy, may I have your cap? I'm afraid I'll get sunstroke out on the water.'

'But you'll be across the river in fifteen minutes.'

'That's true. But it would be a good disguise.'

From behind, Tia's wheelchair squeaked as she rolled closer. 'You two quit whispering. Tom, step back so I can get a clear shot at that dude.'

Looking frightened, Vince put the boat into gear. He started to speak to Tom, then heard the click of the gun's hammer and quickly accelerated. Foam and spray flew up as the boat swept away from the dock.

Tia laughed. 'Good riddance to bad rubbish!' she called, then motioned to Tom and Liz. 'Walk ahead of me into the woods. We're going for a nice ride.'

As Tom started walking, he heard the motor boat drop speed. He glanced back quickly and saw that Vince had stopped outside gunshot-range, and was looking their way. Tom realized he was waiting for them if only they could somehow escape from Tia.

Hoping to keep Tia from noticing Vince, Tom started talking. 'Was the chauffeur the man on the streetcar who pretended I'd stolen his wallet?'

'Yes. Then he drove up to the cabin after you escaped to help search for you.'

Tom looked back at Tia; the pistol rested in her lap so she could turn the wheels of her chair. 'Why'd you park in these woods?'

'So you would'nt recognize my station wagon when you arrived with Vince. Boy, you're certainly one for questions.'

Straight ahead, a long branch dangled low across the narrow road. Tom held on to the branch as he passed; then, when it was bent tight as a spring, he let go.

'Run, Liz!' he shouted.

Tia cried out as the branch whipped back at her. Bending low, Tom plunged through the bushes, hoping desperately that she would not start shooting. There was no sound of gun-fire as he raced out of the trees with Liz and headed for the dock, waving to Vince.

With a roar of power, the motor boat leapt through the water toward them. 'Hurry!' Tom shouted; his heart was hammering, and he was certain that any second he'd hear shots.

Approaching the dock, Vince slowed the engine and yelled something. There was no time for the motor boat to stop; they would have to jump, and Tom tensed every muscle as he waited for the right second.

'Now!' Liz cried.

Together, they jumped through the air and landed safely, but shaken, in the boat. For a moment Tom was winded, then he staggered up as the boat shot away from the dock.

'I did it!' Vince yelled into the wind. 'Victory!'

Tom tried to thank him for the rescue, but was

ignored as Vince stared back at the shore, then started laughing. 'Here come the cops! Right on time!'

Amazed, Tom heard the howl of sirens approaching through the park. At the same time, the station wagon with Tia at the wheel burst out from the trees where it had been hidden. Then, with a screech of metal, it veered to the right and stopped in a cloud of dust. Police cars surrounded the station wagon and, as officers swarmed from the cars, Tia raised her hands in surrender.

'Yahoo!' Vince was beside himself with glee. 'What a sight! That'll teach the dirty double-crosser!'

'But what happened?'

Vince grinned. 'From the start, I planned to trick Tia. We'd arranged where to meet, so I knew her station wagon would be hidden in the woods. Before letting the air out of her wheels so she couldn't drive anywhere, I phoned the Mounties in Canada to say the diamond thief they wanted was in the USA, in Riverside Park.'

Vince paused, chuckling.

'I knew it would take time for the message to get from the Canadian Mounties to the American FBI, and then to the local cops. Before they could reach the park I planned to grab the diamonds from you two, then leave Tia to be arrested while I made my get-away.'

Tom looked at the spectacle of blue and red lights whirling on the police cars in the park. 'Well, Tia is certainly under arrest. But you're still out of luck, Vince.'

'How's that?'

'The police will recover the diamonds from Tia, so you went to all that trouble for nothing.'

Vince grinned happily. 'You think I'm stupid? Don't forget, I never trusted Tia.'

'I don't understand.'

'Think about it kids. If fake diamonds have been used once, then why not twice? And where else have you got crests, besides on your jackets?'

As Tom and Liz stared at Vince, he broke into delighted laughter. Then he seized the caps from their heads, and waved them happily. 'You guessed it! Knowing Tia might try to double-cross me, I told her the diamonds would be in the jacket crests. Those I filled with fakes, and put the real diamonds in the crests on your caps. Wasn't that a fantastic plan?'

Liz shook her head. 'You've also been lucky, Vince.'

'Sure I'm lucky, but so what? We're half-way across this river already, and I'll have plenty of time to get away once we land. The Mounties will never find me, and I'll be rich beyond my wildest dreams!'

Feeling betrayed, Tom looked unhappily at the man he'd liked and trusted. 'When we were going with Tia to her station wagon, I thought you were waiting to rescue us. But you only wanted to get the diamonds from our caps.'

Vince flashed one of his charming smiles. 'Don't take it so hard, Tom. You're still my good buddy, and so is Liz.'

She snorted. 'Everything you say is a lie, Vince.

You robbed your friend Sir Nigel, and would have left him to die in the stables.'

'That old geezer deserved to die! He's got more money than the King of Siam, and he still hoarded the diamonds. Why didn't he give them away to the needy?'

'The needy like you?'

'Sure like me! I'm just an ordinary guy struggling to make a living, and meanwhile Sir Nigel eats caviar in a castle. It made me sick, pretending to become his friend so I could worm out where he'd hidden the diamonds. But don't worry, Liz, I would have let the police know where to find him once I'd reached safety.'

'Other people are greedy, but you're not?'

'That's enough back-talk, young lady. You just like twisting things around so you can look smart.'

'I've been thinking. If you're not an undercover Mountie, then I bet Smythe is.'

'Yes! I'll never forget his face when he was grabbed in the tunnel, and I made my get-away. Don't you see, the Mounties couldn't arrest and search me in Canada because they had no proof, so Smythe's job was to follow me until I tried to cross the border, then have the customs officers conduct a legal search for the diamonds.'

'But they wouldn't have found them anyway.'

'Right again. I'm such an ace guy, I came up with the great idea of having you two carry the diamonds across the border. And you saw what happened. The customs officers searched me closely, but they never thought to check you kids.'

The motor coughed. Vince glanced at it, then

whistled cheerfully as he turned his face to the sun. 'I think I'll visit Florida to work on my tan.'

The motor spluttered again and then cut out completely. Vince dashed to the fuel tank. 'It's empty! That double-crossing woman must have drained out most of the fuel.'

Liz smiled. 'I guess she didn't trust you, Vince.'

'Wipe that smirk off your face, and grab an oar! We're starting to drift.'

Tom looked at the peaceful sunshine and the birds playing in the wind and was surprised by the urgency in Vince's voice. Then he heard a sound that seized him with fear.

Whirling round, he looked down river. 'We're heading for the rapids!'

Liz had already grabbed an oar, and was paddling frantically. 'It's not just the rapids! Look what's beyond them!'

In the distance, where the river appeared to end abruptly, a cloud of spray was rainbowed in the sunshine, marking the deadly place where the river plunged over the Falls to the rocks far below.

Grabbing an oar in his sweating hands, Tom tried to help Liz drive the boat toward the river bank. But the current was too strong, and it carried the boat steadily toward the terrible booming of the rapids.

'It's hopeless!' Vince shouted. 'Drop those oars and hang on!'

A huge rock loomed straight ahead. Tom shut his eyes, then felt the surging water toss the boat away from the rock; cold spray stung his face, and he cried out in fear.

The cry was lost in the thunder of the rapids and Tom could only stare helplessly at the onrushing vision of white water leaping around jagged rocks. The boat veered past a huge boulder, then spun into a sickening whirlpool and as quickly whirled back into the roaring torrent.

Suddenly the rapids ended. Tom's grip on the boat loosened, but his relief was short-lived. He shook the spray from his face and saw that within seconds the ruthless water would carry them to the brink of the Falls.

'That log!' Vince screamed. 'Grab that log when we hit it!'

Ahead there was a log jammed between two boulders. Tom somehow managed to reach up and seize a branch as the boat hit the log. He pulled himself out of the boat just before it was swept away over the Falls.

Stunned, Tom stared at the place where it had disappeared, then he crawled higher up on the log and his heart leapt with relief when he saw Liz and Vince.

'We're safe!' Tom shouted above the deafening sound of the Falls. 'I can't believe it!'

'Safe?' Vince cried. 'You call this safe?'

Tom looked down at the water, which was churning angrily around the log. He shifted his position and the log trembled; with the weight of three people on it, it was likely to break free at any second.

Filled with fear, Tom looked toward the shore. At Table Rock House a crowd was gathering to stare and point; he couldn't believe that only a short while ago he'd been safely standing there, joking about people who'd gone over the Falls.

A tremor passed through the log, and the river foamed higher as if determined to tear it loose from the rock. Tom looked desperately at the crowd on shore, wishing they could somehow help.

Liz cried out and Tom's head snapped round toward the sound, afraid she had fallen in. But his sister was pointing at the sky.

'Look!'

The sun was suddenly obscured, and Tom looked up at a giant RESCUE helicopter. As the huge machine descended slowly out of the sky, he shouted with joy and relief.

'You see?' he called to Vince. 'We really are safe!'

The man's face was pale with fear, and his grip tightened as the whirling blades created a windstorm that shook the log. Above him, a hatch opened in the belly of the helicopter and a rescue basket dropped down. Vince glanced at the basket dangling beside him, then clung even tighter to the log.

'Hurry, Vince!' Liz shouted. 'Get in there before it's too late!'

Vince shook his head, and Tom saw the terror in his eyes. At any moment the log would break loose under their weight; Tom was the next closest to the basket, and he knew he must hurry. Moving carefully from branch to branch along the slippery log, he reached the basket and within seconds had been whirled to the safety of the helicopter, where he was wrapped inside a blanket.

But the danger was not over, and his body shook with anxiety as he watched the basket drop again to the log. 'Hurry, Liz!' he whispered, watching his sister crawl toward the basket.

Reaching it, she stopped to shout something to Vince. When he shook his head, Liz climbed into the basket; the helicopter's winch tightened and very quickly Liz was being bundled inside a blanket by a crew member.

Wiping water from her eyes, Liz looked at the woman. 'Vince is afraid to let go!' she called above the noise of the helicopter.

'I'll help him.' The woman quickly assembled some equipment. 'Vince Winter comes across on TV so big and strong, but now we see the truth!'

'How come you know it's Vince Winter?'

'Oh, I've seen him lots of times on TV.'

As she was lowered in the basket, Tom looked at the man operating the winch. 'How'd you get here so fast?'

'This Rescue chopper is based at Niagara Falls. People are constantly getting into trouble.'

Tom looked through the hatch. The crew member was standing fearlessly on the log, strapping a harness around Vince; then she signalled to the winch operator, and the machine whined.

As the harness ropes tightened, the woman forced Vince to release the branches and he rose away from the log. Spinning slowly like a giant beetle, he was lifted to the helicopter and deposited on the deck.

The crew member followed Vince through the hatch, and quickly undid the harness. When he was free, Vince stumbled to a seat and dropped into it with a sigh of relief.

'I did it, kids!' he said, raising a triumphant hand

to show he was still clutching the baseball caps. 'Despite all that, I saved the diamonds!'

'So what?' Tom replied. 'You're heading for prison, and the jewels will go to Sir Nigel.'

'Sure,' Vince said eagerly. 'But, don't you see, Sir Nigel will have to give me a big reward for saving his diamonds!'

As the helicopter lifted away from the Falls, Liz wrapped the blanket tighter round herself and grinned. 'Boy, Vince, you're better entertainment than a dozen dancing bears. Life won't be the same without you.'

12

As the little plane tilted, Tom felt his stomach lurch.

For a few seconds the plane flew on its side, one wing pointing at the swift blue river below. Then, with a sickening tumble, it was upside down.

'I can't watch!' Liz moaned through her hands.

The plane righted itself, then swept into a narrow canyon over a stretch of seething white water.

'The rapids!' Sir Nigel said. 'Just like I promised you.'

Uncle Henry laughed. 'Haven't you kids had enough of rapids?'

'Yes!'

The plane skimmed low over the water, then the scene was suddenly replaced by the image of a man's gigantic face. As he talked about the need to live in harmony with Nature, Tom wiped his forehead and leaned back in his seat; he'd had enough thrills lately, even second-hand ones.

The *World of Nature* film ended, and the lights went up. Sir Nigel smiled. 'Was it as good as I promised?'

'For sure! Is this really one of the world's largest movie screens?' Tom asked.

'So they say. I see all the shows here, but I confess to sometimes missing the London cinemas.'

'What's Britain like, Sir Nigel?'

'It's marvellous. I'll take you for a visit some day. I'm sure we can find you a spare mystery to solve.'

A few minutes later, the group left the theatre to wander around Ontario Place. Sir Nigel was so pleased to have his diamonds back that he had invited everyone responsible for their recovery to spend the day at the amusement park as his guests. Dexter Valentine and his wife had also been asked to join the party.

'Who's hungry?' Sir Nigel asked, leading the way to a Chinese take-out stand.

Later, laden with chop suey and egg rolls, they found benches with a good view of a lagoon and its procession of floating bands, paddle-boats and other vessels.

'Impossible!' Liz said, reading the message in her fortune cookie. 'I thought you could believe these things.'

'What's it say?'

'I'm about to lose my head over a handsome stranger.'

Uncle Henry smiled. 'Liz is always cool, calm and collected. I'd love to see her lose her head.'

Smythe lifted a sweet-and-sour sparerib with his chopsticks, but they slipped and red sauce spotted his shirt. 'I'd better learn to operate these things before my next undercover assignment.'

'What is it?' Tom asked quickly.

Smythe smiled. 'That's a secret, but I can tell you it's a big change from being a butler.'

'Can you tell us what happened to the original butler at Casa Loma?'

'Sure. He took a holiday at the request of the police, and I replaced him in order to investigate Sir Nigel's disappearance. I understand he'll be back at Casa Loma soon, along with the other servants like poor Hatfield, and I must say he's welcome to the job!'

Uncle Henry looked at Smythe. 'I still don't understand why you quit that day, and left me in the lurch.'

Smythe tried again with the chopsticks, and more sauce splattered. 'Do you recall showing me the diamonds you found in Sir Nigel's desk? When your back was turned, I tested their hardness and quickly discovered they were fakes, which meant the real diamonds had been taken from the castle.'

'But why did you quit?'

'To shadow my chief suspect, Vince Winter. You see, I couldn't tell you the truth about the fake diamonds, in case word got to Vince and he went into hiding. The police wanted him to think his plan had succeeded, so we could nail him at the border-crossing with the diamonds.'

'But the story was in the newspapers.'

'Yes. Unfortunately the papers got on to the story after you two found Sir Nigel, but there was no publicity about us trailing Vince Winter, only a mention of two American suspects.'

Tom blushed. 'I guess it didn't help when I spotted you in the tunnel at Niagara Falls.'

'You're right,' Smythe said, laughing. 'By the time I got out of the tunnel and rushed to join the American police, your motor boat was heading for the Falls. You can imagine how terrible I felt.'

'Well, it all worked out fine in the end.'

A flock of ducks skidded to a landing on the water, and Tom tossed some chow mein in their direction. Then the group walked toward the waterslide, where kids shrieked joyfully as they twisted down long plastic chutes to plunge into a pool.

'Speaking of Casa Loma,' Smythe said, 'it was Vince who recruited a couple of petty crooks to pose as a chauffeur and a blacksmith, and Tia who made sure they were hired.'

'You know,' Tom said, 'I should have realized that Vince and Tia were secretly their bosses.'

'Why's that?'

'Well, I'd seen the tracks of Tia's wheelchair at Fort York; then the same marks were on the driveway at the cabin where I was a prisoner. Another tip-off came at the phone booth on the country road, when the driver of the station wagon didn't chase me. I should have realized that meant the driver was Tia, who couldn't run because of her disability.'

'But what about Vince?'

'At first I couldn't understand why I had been grabbed on the streetcar,' Tom said. 'It was only when the blacksmith asked me where the diamonds were hidden that I began to realize what was going on. But who could have told him that I had guessed where the diamonds were? Only three people knew I had a theory.'

Mrs Valentine smiled. 'My husband and I were two of them.'

Tom nodded. 'And Vince was the third.'

'But we're Americans, like Vince and Tia. How could you tell we weren't the villains?'

'Two main reasons. First, because it was Vince who arranged for me to take the streetcar and so set me up for the grab. I should have realized it that day when the kidnappers brought me back to Toronto and I learned that no streetcar goes anywhere near Casa Loma.'

'And the second reason?'

'Way back at the beginning, when Hatfield disappeared from the study, Vince said he'd contact the police. But they never showed up—obviously because Vince didn't want them poking around.'

Smythe shook his head. 'Vince and Tia figured they had covered every angle, but there's always an unexpected event that makes a crime go wrong.'

'Poor Vince,' Liz said. 'He won't like giving up his fancy clothes for prison stripes.'

'Or his digital watch,' Tom added. 'By the way, that was another clue that I should have picked up.'

'How so?'

'At the cabin I heard the blacksmith talking about

one of his bosses having a twenty-four hour watch. I should have remembered that Vince was always consulting his digital watch.'

The group was drawn by loud cries toward the children's village, where they stopped for a moment to watch the wild battles in the water-wars area and the foam swamp, until they became aware of even louder screams coming from the distance.

'What's that?' Liz said.

Sir Nigel frowned. 'It's coming from the Forum, where they have open-air shows, but I can't imagine what's happening. Nobody was screaming when I saw the Toronto Symphony there.'

'Let's investigate!'

Hurrying toward the noise, they saw a canopy-roof stretched over grassy slopes and seats which surrounded a stage; all around the stage, police officers were struggling to hold back thousands of hysterical girls who were trying to reach a young singer.

'Big deal,' Liz said. 'It's a rock concert. Look at all those crazy girls, going nuts over some no-talent pretty face.'

'It's somebody new,' Tom said. 'I've never heard of him before.'

'How do you know his name?'

'It's on that sign. He's called Nick Nalini.'

'*Nick Nalini!* Are you kidding me?'

'Nope. Read the sign for yourself.'

Liz trembled. 'It really is Nick Nalini! Why didn't someone tell me?'

Uncle Henry laughed. 'But he's just some no-talent pretty face, Liz.'

'Don't ever say that about Nick Nalini! He's the most perfect creature ever born, and he's *right here!*'

Liz started walking toward the Forum, then she broke into a run and disappeared into the seething mass of fans.

Sir Nigel laughed. 'The fortune cookie was right after all. Liz has lost her head over a handsome stranger, but I'm sure she'll survive the experience. I just hope her ear-drums survive that music!'

'You know,' Smythe said, 'the blacksmith should have made you listen to Nick Nalini records in the stables. I'm sure you would have revealed the diamonds' hiding-place in no time.'

Sir Nigel smiled. 'You could be right. One's bravery has its limits.'

Irene studied him thoughtfully. 'I admire you, Sir Nigel. You really stood up to those crooks.'

'I must say the admiration is mutual, my dear. Now, don't you think it's time for the others to learn your secret role in this affair?'

Irene nodded, then turned to Uncle Henry with embarrassed eyes. 'I must apologize for letting you believe I was a maid at Casa Loma. You see, I was under strict orders not to reveal my true identity to anyone, including you.'

'You mean you were never one of the servants?'

She shook her head. 'I'm also a Mountie, and, like Smythe, I was at the castle as an undercover investigator.'

For a moment there was silence, then Uncle Henry laughed with surprise and delight. 'You had me completely fooled! I must say I was very surprised when you left Casa Loma without saying good-bye.'

'I felt badly about that, but it was impossible to tell you why I was leaving. I couldn't risk having the truth leak to the people I was after.'

'Who were they?'

'The blacksmith and the chauffeur. I'm happy to report we arrested them early this morning.'

Uncle Henry smiled at Irene. 'Hey, you're really something! How about having dinner with me tonight?'

'I'd love to.'

Looking pleased, Uncle Henry turned to Tom with a wink. 'When we get home to Winnipeg, nobody will believe everything that's happened to us. Especially if word gets out that it all ended with me dating a good-looking Mountie!'

Tom laughed. 'Your secret is safe with me, Unc.'